For Karl & utopias.

Metamorfabulous

In a world that's almost familiar, a resourceful woman considers renting out her sons for their peculiar skill in causing mirth and merriment. Sounds from a circus and a prelapsarian sky are nearly muffled by the plantation blinds of a regular suburban house. Inside, a regular suburban woman, morally torn and easy to dismiss. And on the other side of a wall in the backyard, on the golf-course side, there's opportunity for a quest—to right a wrong and find a key, to save the stolen and to start anew. A shot to tidy a former global disaster lies just on the other side of the beige brick wall, there in a literary elsewhere with its other-world music and colors and special drinks.

I opened the door to *The Evolutionary Revolution* and almost knew where I was. A place familiar-yet-strange. The prettiest girl in town is light and lithe and her name is "Sylvia," which means "she that inhabits the woods," and her last name is "Sylph," which means "she that inhabits the air." She also inhabits the suburbs, a simultaneously airy and materially earthbound place.

In this consciously formed and unconsciously misformed realm, which is made in part by stories, opposites don't cancel each other out. Under the sea, inside the moon, in a tract home. There's an origin egg and a beast guarding a final destination at the center of an impossible maze. There's an underwater otherworld as awe-ful as a madman's cave. There's a freakshow, a secret, and a lost memory. There's a powerful Council and a Council to keep it in check. There's war, there's global warming, teenage girls with powers of deception, and Bubblicious. There's an angel or a mortal who falls or climbs down into an underworld of the unconscious. Recognizable features of fables and myth splay across the first pages of *The Evolutionary Revolution*. Horatio Algiers and PT Barnum bed down with Aesop and Homer.

The plural narrator is convincing. I'm reminded that this is part myth, part true. I am told there is a goal—an order to restore. I am oriented within a tradition. I am told to believe I know where I am.

But just as I snuggle in, one of Hoang's narrative roulette wheel turns and I fall into a sea of uncertainty, just like Mama Sylph. The story spins and flings its characters out of their trajectories, whimsically fucking with the story's facts at every turn.

The purpose of myth is to detail what changed and why. The purpose of a fable is to help sculpt change, that is, to dramatize common causes of nasty effects, warning a reader what behavior to avoid. Myth is about the past, fable is about the future. Because myth animates the inanimate planets, we're able to choose whether they wanted to live or to die. Fables are peopled with animals in pants and bow-ties to keep the lessons from feeling too didactic. A talking fox who wanders beneath a cluster of grapes and calls them sour for being out of reach is easier to countenance than the infant-eating cannibal Tantalus in Hades.

There is a dormant, desiccated moon, but no talking animals in *The Evolutionary Revolution*. There are plenty of other mutants and their mythical forebears. The freakish boys of the suburbs are throwbacks to the sea-dwelling conjoined twins of yore. In fact, in *The Evolutionary Revolution*, conjoined characters blossom like a hundred two-headed flowers. There are evil twins, sure, but there are also pretty ones, dead ones, sorrowful ones, and dreamers. And while some are not physically joined—they may even be separated by time and space—they are nonetheless conjoined.

This proliferation inspired me to investigate the history and symbology of Siamese Twins, and I learned about Chang and Eng, the hardworking brothers who lived the American Dream. Back before the Civil War, Chang and Eng, the original "Siamese Twins," provided a brotherly metaphor for state unity in opposition to the separatists. Hailing from exotic Siam, they were different enough for American audiences to look at without feeling implicated, yet similar enough to serve a symbolic purpose: to separate the North from the South. To separate them would be to murder both entities. So, even during this period of intense public anxiety about the threat of grotesque genetic mutation via miscegenation, the twins' unification became a visual metaphor of healthy-if-uncomfortable togetherness, which was good for the abolitionists in the Senate. But the brothers also portrayed the freakishness of unions against nature. The twins would not be torn asunder, even as they coupled (quadrupled?) with their wives.

An American myth begins with: *E pluribus Unum*.

An American fable ends with: *Let your freak flag fly!*

Not exactly a side note, but in 1832, after touring much of the world as nature's oddities, the brothers and their families settled on a plantation in North Carolina, where they became even wealthier through the labor of thirty-three slaves. Incest and fidelity and lust and repulsion are not such strange bedfellows in both domestic and public politics.

A special echo chamber of the imagination resonates with the perverse laughter of hypocrites and chimera. This chamber is a grotto for upsetting the boundaries of certainty and selfhood. It is the site of the grotesque.

In one of my favorite books, *The Secret Life of Puppets*, Victoria Nelson describes how the known origins of the Western grotesque trace back to the fifteenth century when Italian antiquarians dug up Nero's Domus Aurea and found on its walls "murals depicting strange hybrid monsters of a style in vogue in the first century after Christ—a style Horace had mocked in *Ars Poetica* for its fantastic juxtapositions (a horse's neck with a man's head, a woman's body with a fish's tail) as 'dreams of a sick person's mind.'"[1] Italian painters, including Raphael, were inspired by these fevered dreams. In the following century, the style *alla grotesca* became very popular among European nobility; every garden had a grotto. Visitors went to hide away in these fun and scary antechambers to meditate in the cool stillness. There, they could ponder the divine and misshapen wonders adorning the grotto's back wall. Behind them, the grotto's mouth designated a visible threshold between a fear aesthetically articulated and contained and the more familiar danger outside the cave.

A grotesque is a combinatory creature that undoes.

The Evolutionary Revolution is a grotesque of conjoined, incestuous fables and myths. The offspring is the moral of the story. Yet Hoang's moral is not Aesop's. There won't be a clearly moral moral. And the evolutionary revolution, which changed everything or will change everything, may or may not be a wish

---

[1] Victoria Nelson, *The Secret Life of Puppets*, Harvard University Press, 2001. 2.

and a fear. This moral is scary and fun, and it doesn't serve to strengthen my ego.

Sylph sounds a lot like "self."

The grotesque dismantles a sense of self, undermining the notion of a contained self that is separate from a sublime yet banal disorder.

In the book, order is established, then overturned without explanation. Even the all-knowing narrators are thrown off course as they relay the story's shifting facts. They admit, "We are trying our hardest to keep things straight, but we are becoming confused and frustrated with all these tales, and we are trying to decipher the most truthful history, but with so many variations, time itself becomes arbitrary and even the players have lost a certain distinction […]." (147)

As the narrators become more uncertain, I forget that I know where I am, in a world that's almost familiar. Am I being interpolated by the plural narrator? Who is telling this story? To what end and under what duress? Could it be we all are under the spell of the wily nymphet, Sylvia Sylph? The narrators confide, "She knows we are at her mercy for snippets of information, things we couldn't possibly learn ourselves, things she changes on a whim because she can, because sometimes, she likes to throw us off with a simple snap." (160)

And in literature, as sometimes in life, it's a scary kind of fun to be manipulated by a pretty girl, who changes the game on a whim. That's how Sylvia rolls; she likes to put her spin on things. You could call her whimsical tactic of changing the story willy-nilly revolutionary. It changes everything, forever.

You could call a convincing agent of change like Sylvia's snap a mutagen. A mutagen is a physical, chemical, or conceptual agent that alters the desire of an organism and thus increases the frequency of mutations. Another example of a mutagen is the carcinogen tritium. Another is the word "No."

Like back in the old days, when, according to the narrators, the mythical Evolution Council decreed to a group of conjoined thugs, *No, you may not be separated.*

To be drawn into the gorgeousness of the tragic is to become a kind of mutant. On the day the Evolution Council says no to a request for autonomy, man falls into a sea of sorrow. Here, man is a woman, a kind one. Pasted-shut eyes and ugly wings physically articulate her species and gender. She is a grotesque. Here, the author isn't interested in collaboration with her readers. She's the generic/genetic engineer introducing mutagens and forcing mutations, as if this tricky fable were for her own pleasure as well as ours. For the reader it is again a scary sort of fun to be led and led astray by Hoang. As if its mutagens are happily recombining like rabbits, the moral of this fable keeps contradicting itself, as if by chance.

Evolution or revolution, chance or choice, myth or fable, past or future? And then, Ding!

{Please turn the page.}

The known world will be overturned. Turning the page will prompt a fall, a recognizable warning: Don't fly too close to the sun! Don't open the special closet with the special key! Don't let curiosity be your guide! This time falling will feel like swooping through a deep lightless sea. Ordinary direction will no longer make sense. This narrative space is vast and omnidirectional. It is a maze with no prize egg at the center.

Not even human wings offer a shot at transcendence, tongue-in-cheek or otherwise. Wings that don't fly are nothing but ugly red flippers. Wings that don't fly are not made for getting to heaven.

There's no final resting place with fluffy-cloud bedding in sight.

There's only the narrators' rather desperate authoritative tone in lieu of sage advice. This plural narrator (who always makes sure to include us) reminds, "This is our story to manipulate until we no longer control it. This is, in fact, our duty. Memory can only linger if it undergoes perpetual evolution." (108)

This is also the novel's explanation of its own fierce watery way.

The Evolutionary Revolution is like a moving grotto made of seawater instead of stone. Its chimera cavort, distort, and combine at Hoang's leisure. These monstrosities are unreliable in their movements and hard to keep straight. Myth and fable metamorphose for no reason at all, or if there is any reason, it's buried beneath layers and layers of reconfabulation.

Once, back when I first opened the book, a narrator who seemed to be a neutral guide oriented me to the novel's carnivals and angels. Once, I was directed to believe I knew exactly where I was, in a fabulous myth. That was a trap, and a good one.

Once, a set of two men irrevocably joined was a hopeful metaphor for the United States. As the young nation was falling apart over the issues of slavery and state's rights, Chang and Eng were living proof of that which could not be put asunder. Now, in an era of world-uniting capitalist globalization, Hoang animates hoards of conjoined twins that share names and change roles. Their stage is an omnidirectional realm that, like a grotto, is mysterious, inviting, and distorting. Alternately, their stage is the equally unnavigable sphere of attachment and aversion, the family home.

The Evolutionary Revolution is a revolt against the oversimplification of fable and myth. Hoang's ethical imperative manifests in the story's insistence on its readers' curiosity and flexibility.

This grotesque *does* end with a moralizing moral: Mama Sylph (you'd never guess) is you, all fallen and splashing.

So swim.

Anna Joy Springer

Los Angeles, California
2010

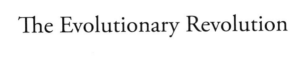

The Evolutionary Revolution

Carnival

Her husband never wanted to display their boys like that, but Mama Sylph, she didn't mind. She was a smart woman, always looking for the quickest way to make the most honest buck. Honest was the key word. Mama Sylph was a good, Christian woman. She didn't believe in selling her body, or her boys' body, for that matter. She was adamant about this, but when the head carnie came asking about the Sylph boys, she listened carefully. She told the head carnie they were a good, Christian family, one who didn't believe in selling their bodies, that was prostitution. But the head carnie said he certainly didn't believe in prostitution either, that the carnival was, in its own very special way, a good, Christian organization. She had it all wrong, the whole world had it wrong, and it was her duty as a good, Christian woman to be understanding.

Mama Sylph wasn't easily fooled, but she listened as carefully as she could, digressing from the truth with small liberties until she believed the carnival offered a space to display her boys, her very special boys, as nature's, no, God's artwork. Mama Sylph listened until words like freak and sideshow dissolved. Her boys were unique sculptures, each detail added by God Himself, but she didn't let the head carnie take her boys away. No, even though they needed the money, Mama Sylph didn't bend. She stayed strong.

Years later, months after Papa Sylph injected air into his veins, she reconsiders the carnival. She remembers the way the carnie man talked, how his voice was melted sugar, and then.

Water World

A long time ago, long before man walked, the earth was a sphere of solid liquid. Above, the atmosphere existed as it does today, only cleaner, much cleaner. The surface of the water did not splash waves because there was nothing for the water to collide with except air. A long time ago, the ocean was so clear that man flying in the air could see directly through the water, straight to the other side of the planet, except back then, man had horrible vision. Only the rare, exceptional man could even see the surface of the water because her eyes were so small. As such, man was forced to rely on her other senses, such as memory, kindness, and dream interpretation.

There was, in fact, a fairly extensive period of time, approximately an era or two before the Evolutionary Revolution, when man could hardly open her eyelids out of sensitivity to hydrogen. The moment she opened her eyes, they would sear with such ferocity that as a sub-species, man decided to never use her eyes again. As such, men would flap their little red wings to stay as stationary as possible while friends used strands of hair and mucous to seal the eyes shut.

It is said man started using her eyes again when a young girl named Emily heard the song of a merman twinkling from the surface of the water. She'd never dreamt of him before. She had no memory of his voice, but his song contained such sadness that out of kindness, she pried her eyes open with the tips of her talons, using all the force she could, and from those eyes, she saw deep into the ocean, deep into the most tortured song.

Opened Eyes

Emily's eyes, being unaccustomed to hydrogen, crackled, but she was unafraid. Her eyes, being unaccustomed to wind and sight, automatically barricaded themselves behind moist lids, behind darkness, but she, being the bravest of men, was determined to maintain strength.

It is said the merman's song seeped its melody deep into her liver, where all impurities are filtered, and the contamination of her body by his song made her pry her eyes open with her toes, and when her eyes opened and she could finally see, she fell deep into the merman's song. It is said she was the first to fall, but this cannot be substantiated. Although she is the first recorded man to be lured by a merman's song, oral stories offer many more examples of men who have ripped cement from their eyes, begging other men to bite off the seal, so they could finally see what kind of being created melodies of such penetrating sadness.

It is said mermen dream only in shadow and light. Shapes are never definitive and sound is muted. It is said mermen actively chose to dream this way. Mermen were particularly divisive and because they knew man above the water could not see but relied solely on her other senses, mermen created dreams man above water could not navigate. It was a strategic move.

The day Emily divided the atmosphere, falling freely, hydrogen cutting her freshly opened eyes, she was unafraid. She somehow knew she would survive, that in the water, her eyes would no longer hurt, that his song would always be near, and even though she, our young heroine, wasn't frightened, we know better. We know that even though she's strong and unafraid, she ought to be. Yes, she should have known better, and even now, even now as she's sinking lower than man has sunk since they lived under water, she should know better than to think she can still be a heroine, but she doesn't.

A Development of Wings

The day Chloe Henklemeyer woke to find wings on her thighs, two pairs on each leg, a total of eight miniature wings desperately fluttering, she tried to pull them off. The day she woke to find a pair of wings on her legs, neither fully synchronized, the movement hectic, she was calm. Sure, she didn't expect to wake up one day and find wings on her legs, and sure, wings weren't supposed to sprout like this, on her thighs of all places, but she was unruffled. Though she wasn't opposed to the idea of growing wings, she certainly didn't expect them to grow on her thighs. She'd imagined wings would grow some place elegant—on her back or even her ankles, like that Greek god—but still she was surprisingly calm. And sure, you hear the word *wings*, and you think of something small and sweet, like a moth or a butterfly or even a cute, little bird. Or conversely, you think of something strong and powerful, like an eagle or an angel, but no, not her wings. The day Chloe Henklemeyer woke to find wings on her legs, she extended her right hand to touch one of the wings shivering on her inner thigh. These wings which just appeared, just like that, were something entirely different than what she would have imagined. They didn't have feathers; they barely had skin. They were red and raw, like something formed in an embryonic sac but were forced to hatch before they'd had a chance to fully develop. Chloe extended her right hand to touch them. She was sure they would feel like mucous. She was certain they'd feel ugly, have the texture of hideousness.

But they were smooth, and they wiggled. Chloe Henklemeyer closed her right then her left hand around the small wings attached to the inside of her thigh and tightened her grip. She closed first her right eye then her left, blinking deeply, clamped her jaw, and pulled with all her force.

The day she woke to find wings on her thighs, she learned these wings were most certainly attached to her. She couldn't remove them by pulling. She considered a saw, some scissors, a wrench. Of course, she couldn't really endure the pain of a saw, and scissors seemed inhumane, and the wrench, well, what could she possibly do with a wrench to remove an excess of wings? That day she woke, she quickly learned she couldn't walk with these four wings scraping each other on the insides of her thighs. She learned she couldn't wear tight pants. She couldn't, in fact, wear any pants at all, but she learned to control their movement by blinking to her heartbeat.

The day she woke to find wings on her thighs, she thought she would be able to fly. After she relearned how to walk, she climbed to the top of her tussled bed and saw how dirty her apartment was, but she ignored it. She ignored the room, the sound, her insecurity, the movement of her heart beating more quickly, with more spirit. She stood on top of her bed that day she woke to find wings on her thighs, and she knew if she only tried hard enough, she would be able to fly. And so she jumped, and upon jumping, she knew something wasn't quite right. During her momentary journey down to the ground, she quickly learned how wrong she was. She learned that the creator created her without any sense of utility or function. She learned that sometimes people wake from long nights to find new appendages that do absolutely nothing.

Two-Headed Boy

There's a song about a two-headed boy, but it's not about Eliot and Sylvester Sylph, even though Eliot thinks it is. Of course, Sylvester disagrees.

Eliot romanticizes the love story, how people like them can have girlfriends.

Sylvester argues this particular two-headed boy is imprisoned in a freaking jar, showcased as a freak.

Eliot says, "How's that any different than us?"

Sylvester says, "Eliot, you're my best friend, my brother, my twin, and you're attached to me, and I just can't understand how the hell you're so fucking stupid."

Eliot says, "OK, so we're not stuck in a jar, but we're stuck in a carnival so how's that any different really? We may as well be stuck in a jar, Sly. We may as well be dead."

Sylvester says nothing.

Eliot realizes he's just made his brother's point for him.

The Earth and the Moon

A long time ago, long before man walked upright, the earth was filled with water. It was a sphere of pure ocean. During this era, man flew in the atmosphere with tiny wings attached to her thighs. Back then, man as a sub-species was kind. She was gentle, never provoking arguments, never killing other beings for sustenance, or even pleasure. It's said that man's language didn't account for cruelty. Acts of aggression were nameless and silent, as if they never existed. During the day, man flew over the ocean, playfully chattering about this or that, and at night, she slept on the moon. Of course, the moon was much closer to the earth than it is today. Depending on the time of day, the moon could be as close as a hundred feet or so away from the closest cloud. Back before man walked upright, back when the earth was filled with water, the moon brimmed with vegetation. Being as arable as it was, man used the moon as a very large farm. After flying around the earth all day, man would return to the moon and work for a couple of hours. Because man was so agreeable, she never fought about who would do what and where. Her work was simple and quick, and as a united force, they grew fruits of unimaginable sweetness and their greens were darker than envy.

After their two hours of daily work, man gorged herself and slept unwaking through the night. Although her days were spent on earth, she lived on the moon. She called the moon home.

The Secret Life of Eliot Sylph

He cannot be blamed. Eliot cannot be blamed when late at night, while his brother is securely dreaming, he closes his eyes and sends his brother into a maze of sleep, a labyrinth intricately unsolvable. Eliot determines that Sylvester cannot wake until he has safely found his way out. He doesn't want his brother to die; he just wants a little time to himself. He knows Sylvester can break any code, he's brilliant like that, so he doesn't have any regrets. When Eliot sends his brother into this mystical landscape, he closes his own eyes, imagining a world without Sylvester. When he opens his eyes, he's no longer attached to his brother. He has his own body, his own hands, his own action. Eliot stands up without the difficulty of navigating movement between two distinct minds, and he feels light. He stands up and walks to a new closet, one he has never seen before, and inside this closet hangs clothes made for single boys, not double boys, and he puts on a new self.

Eliot Sylph dresses slowly, savoring each singular motion. When he leaves his room, he touches Sylvester's head, just to check he's still saturated in amazement. Eliot walks away from his brother, his brother who is now only a head. Eliot thinks maybe tonight will be the night he leaves this life behind forever—it's so much easier being a single boy— he thinks Sylvester would be happy to stay in that labyrinth, and Eliot twists the doorknob of the front door locked.

The Edge

At the end of this winding road, there's an egg. It's a large egg, probably three feet high, a foot and a half wide. The egg is dirty, weathered white, almost leathery, with red freckles. It doesn't seem right, its having red spots. An egg should have spots but not red ones. The red is a bright red, the color of hydrants and stop signs, and its brightness glows. Inside the egg, there's an intense tornado of hot, spinning violently, unrepentant. Every couple of minutes, the egg's shell convulses. Whatever's inside, whatever it is in all that heat, it wants out.

At the edge of this very winding road, there is an egg. Except it isn't a road and it isn't winding. Sylvester Sylph thinks it should be a road twisting with smooth curves, but this isn't the case at all. The road moves sharply, turning perfectly perpendicular, completely straight, even when it turns. And it isn't a road. It's more of path, but it doesn't seem like it's ever been walked on before, as if this were the very first time it's been touched, except that it's groomed, neatly, covered in an inch of pedicured grass. As Sylvester Sylph stands there, looking down where his feet freshly imprint the grass, the weight of his body soaking through his shoes slowly sinking down, he thinks this path is perfect for him. He thinks how perfectly he fits here, a single boy, no longer a double boy, a two-headed freak show, and it's only here on this path that he's become a single boy. And single boy Sylvester knows he's dreaming. In this dream, standing on this covered road, a road with lavish vines braided into a shadowy cave, making everything just a few shades darker, Sylvester Sylph begins to walk, careful to turn corners with precision, careful not to cut himself with sharp movement, and he thinks he would much prefer a winding path, and suddenly, the squared angles bend until they twist into smooth curves, and he thinks he'd much prefer dirt to grass. And as he walks, dust swims around his single boy ankles.

The Incorporation of the Story of Salt into Today's Mythology

No one argues that the ocean was not always salty. No one would even think to make this argument. No one rational at least. Even though no one alive today even remembers a time when the ocean wasn't salty, nor has anyone heard any stories of a time when the ocean wasn't so salty, still, no one argues against its saltiness.

If someone were to argue against it or to say their great-great-granddaddy told them a story about a day when the sea wasn't salty, we'd say they were full of shit.

The truth is no one could have any sort of memory about it, not even through oral tradition. But it's true. There was a time when the ocean wasn't salty. It's just not in our memory. If it were in our memory, it would be a false fairy tale, a fake myth, something made up to account for the salt in the ocean that bears no resemblance to the actual course of events that catalyzed the incorporation of salt into a mass of clean, untainted water. Any story about the saltiness of the ocean is a lie, we can say that much for sure. Of course, much like Shakespeare's typewriting monkeys, we're sure that any day now, one of these permutations of myth will turn out to be correct, turn out to be exactly as it happened, though the next time the story is told, something will have changed, and the whole thing will once again be as unright as it was in the first place.

Eliot Goes to the Big City

Eliot Sylph doesn't know where to go. He barely knows how to walk without another boy attached to him. He lacks equilibrium. He teeters like a drunk man. Eliot makes it all the way to the mailbox at the end of the driveway before he loses his footing and falls down. He looks at his scraped shin and wonders if Sylvester is bleeding too, if Sylvester, in his dream, can feel what Eliot feels. Eliot quickly gets to his feet. He doesn't want to miss this chance. It may be his only chance to be a single boy.

Eliot teaches himself how to run, and he runs for miles until he reaches suburbia. Then, he runs more miles until he is smack in the center of a city. He isn't sure what city it is, but it's filled with noise and vibrations he isn't used to. The Sylph boys only know the atmosphere of home, carnivals, and hospitals. When they ride in cars, they are locked in the trunk so no one can hurt them with stares and pointed fingers. When they ride in the car, they can't breathe.

Eliot looks around the city. It's big. He sees women like on television only they're three-dimensional. He can touch them. He's got a big hard-on and he doesn't hide it. This is his one chance so he takes it. He wonders if Sylvester can feel all this and smiles thinking how jealous he would be.

Eliot Makes a Big Choice

Of course Eliot doesn't get laid. He does, however, get slapped many times.

Eliot looks at his watch. It's only been a few hours, but he isn't sure how time works in dreams, if maybe Sylvester has been stuck in that maze for too long.

Eliot stays until the band plays its last song, then he leaves the bar, disappointed. He feels like a hero, like he's Odysseus, waging war for ten years only to endure another ten years just to return home, and Eliot wishes it could stay like this forever. He doesn't miss his brother. When he reaches the edge of the city's downtown, he pauses.

He considers the possibility of staying out here, of forgetting about Sylvester, but this is an experiment and he doesn't know what would happen if Mama or Sylvia woke Sylvester up by mistake, if he would die without a body. So Eliot lifts his left foot and crosses the street that will take him past the highway to the street he will follow for miles and miles as it turns into the street and turns into the street that curves into the street that holds his house where his mama is sleeping and his little sister Sylvia is sleeping and his brother is sleeping without a body to call his own.

The Heroine

Once, there is a beautiful girl with a face completely askew. Her eyes are set too close together, and when she was smaller, she wanted to wear glasses, but no pair of glasses would stay on her nose, it being so flat. This, of course, is hardly a problem because she doesn't need to wear glasses. Her vision is perfect, but it is the potentiality of one day needing glasses—glasses that would simply refuse to fit her face—that makes her sad.

Her lips are bubblegum pink, the color of Bubblicious or some other kind of bubblegum flavored gum. It's a color that only comes from tubes or candy, but for her, it's natural, and its naturalness is disturbing. Still, she's breathtaking. She's beautiful and when she speaks, it's soft. When she speaks, people bend lower and lower to her bubblegum mouth to hear her words. When she speaks, you expect to smell that bubblegum saturated right into her words. When she speaks, she covers her mouth, embarrassed of the sounds she makes. She does this, and it's wonderful. She laughs and people stop moving.

Sylvia and Time

It is not necessarily that Sylvia can stop movement by smiling. Certainly no one, not even the most powerful or gifted beings, can barter with time. Long ago, long before the days of prophets and storytellers, long before any Council for anything was created, much longer than anything we could even conceive of, it was established that time was allowed to move as she wants, however she wants. If time wanted to jump hula hoops, she could. No one could stop her and no one could persuade her to do otherwise, not even the charming Miss Sylvia Sylph, for although she is quite charming, she can't stop time.

Although she can't stop time, Sylvia Sylph can do something fairly similar. With her little pretty head, she can drill into anyone's head and manipulate them into believing that time has stopped. She can do this and so much more. If she wanted to, she could make every person on earth believe time has stopped, or any number of other things, if she wanted, but of course, she doesn't want to.

Luckily, Sylvia Sylph is a very nice girl. We are all very lucky that little Sylvia Sylph is such a nice girl indeed.

Stanley Sylph Gets Sent to the Corner

Back before he changed his name from Stanley Sylph to Papa Sylph to Stanley Henklemeyer, back before he could control his powers, back when he was just a boy, he was always getting into trouble. His mama always put him in the corner, though every time he went to the corner, it was only for a couple seconds because his mama just couldn't punish such a sweet boy, at least not for very long. When Stanley Sylph was a boy, he had to work hard to get into another person's head. He had to practice, and his mama was the perfect subject. He'd time himself. He'd do something to get into trouble. The moment his nose touched the wall, he'd press the top right button on his new battery-powered digital watch. Then he'd concentrate, smashing his eyelids until he was crying and his mama was repenting her harsh punishment. It wasn't long before his mama started ignoring his wrongdoing altogether, like it was invisible to her.

It is hard to have such powers as a boy. It's hard not to misuse them.

The Real Mermen

Mermen are not as contemporary people think of them. Through a complex series of bastardized fairy tales, many conceive of mermen as cute, cuddly, half-men, half-fish. This is simply not true.

Mermen live underwater. This is about as much as they have in common with modern notions of mermen. Real mermen do not have scales or elaborate iridescent tails, and they certainly don't use these non-existent tails to flitter around the ocean, singing sweet little merman songs. There is nothing precious about mermen. They do not have flowing golden locks, and as for the most common misconception, there are no merwomen or mermaids, if you prefer the romanticized term. They don't exist. All mermen are called mermen, and they are at once both male and female and neither. They have sex organs but do not use them.

Mermen do indeed sing songs, but they are not sweet songs. They do not soothe or relax. No, mermen use songs as bait to catch men. Most often, these men are killed and eaten or tortured, killed and eaten, or some combination of that sort. The songs the mermen sing are deep and voluptuous, the way sound was intended to be heard, the way sound is never heard anymore. Because the merman's song was so hypnotic, it is said the Evolution Council eradicated the bodily structures that could create that wavelength of sound, but mermen are resilient and it did not take long for them to find substitutes in their own bodies to make songs deeper than movement, fuller than knowledge, to lure men from the skies into their ocean. It did not take long before just one man fell. After the first man fell and the mermen continued their calls upward into the atmosphere, men began to fall as if their little red wings could no longer hold a weight so burdensome.

The Twentieth Birthday

The day Chloe Henklemeyer woke to find wings on her thighs, it was her birthday. Her twentieth birthday. The day she woke to find wings on her thighs, she struggled to remove them. Then, she tried to make use of them. Then, resigned, she slept.

While she slept, her dreams, generally vivid and lush with color, were dampened to shades of shadow and light. Her dreams, usually noxious with sound, were muted, but not completely silent. Despite her dream irregularity, she was certain she would wake and her wings would be gone. Even in her subconscious state, she willed it. Even sleeping, she was unafraid.

She woke the day after the day she woke to find wings on her thighs, and the wings were still there. That's when she started to panic. She reconsidered surgical options, removal devices, nothing seemed too illogical. She took a wrench and started beating her own wings. She hit them for as long as she could stand the pain. Unmarked, they trembled, so she lifted the wrench and slammed it down again and again. She sat on her hardwood floor, legs split uncomfortably open, lavender red splattered over her naked skin. When she could no longer lift the weight of the wrench, her head spilled over her body and she cried. Her legs were bruised and bleeding around the base of the wings, but the wings, they were intact.

The next day, Chloe tried a saw. The day after that, she suffocated them with thick rubber bands. The day after that, she used a needle and punctured a thousand holes into each wing. They would bleed momentarily then heal themselves whole again.

One of those early days, she remembered her girl days, the days when she daydreamed that she would one day grow to have wings on her legs. She remembered the day her mother turned twenty, how Chloe had made wheat pancakes and honeydew and freshly squeezed orange juice and coffee with cream but no sugar, how just before she brought the food up to her mother's room, her mother had screamed. It was a scream that sounded too familiar, muted, like it was made through a cashmere gag.

Her mother died that day, and Chloe saw the wings only briefly, for a second or two, but they remained in her, repressed, until she was putting holes in her own wings, the wings she remembered she'd wanted for so long.

The day her mother turned twenty, Chloe went to live with her grandfather, and he alone raised her, his wife having died when she turned twenty, the day she woke to find wings on her thighs, two pairs per leg, a total of eight miniature wings desperately fluttering.

Man's Senses

Although man couldn't open her eyes while flying, she could see through her other senses. Movement was never dangerous for man. It was interaction with others that could jeopardize her, which was why man petitioned the Evolution Council for three additional senses.

Man was very beautiful and her utter kindness was enough for any being to permit special favors, even the Evolution Council. Not surprisingly, however, mermen were immune to these feelings.

When man decided to stop using her eyes, to seal them shut with hair and mucous, she petitioned the Evolution Council for three new senses in lieu of this one very useful sense. Each new sense had different rules and particularities. Memory, for instance, dealt not only with their memories but also the memories of those no further than 50 meters away. Through this sense, she could see the pasts of others, their characters and development. The key word here is see. She could see into their pasts with perfect vision.

Kindness worked in a much different way. Man herself was a kind creature, and she invoked kindness in others. If this doesn't seem like a sense, it's because it isn't. The kindness man requested from the Evolution Council was an ability to interpret kindness through heat. If a being was kind, he would emanate great heat. If he wasn't, he'd cause man's flesh to restrict with coldness. Those in between, man could feel in color, but this wasn't something she requested from the Council. This was a skill she refined over centuries of work.

The Evolution Council had little difficulty allowing for the first two senses, but they were hesitant to permit dream interpretation. Man's draft of both petition and proposal for dream interpretation offered too many loopholes, too many possibilities, from manipulation to simple interpretation, but in the end, the Council approved the whole package.

At this point in time, the Evolution Council was not as sophisticated as it is today. Back then, they would either ratify or reject. Modifications were impossible. Given this burden, the powerful Evolution Council felt it had no choice but to approve all three senses for man.

The Red Freckled Egg

The egg is hot, as though inside it lived a swirling liquid fire. Inside, there's a whirlwind of melted hot center, floating in a thick cooling layer of cashmere. The porous nature of cashmere allows little bits of what's in the middle to seep to the surface, or exterior, of the egg, burning red spots onto the weathered shell.

The few who have touched this egg testify to feeling what they are certain is a heartbeat, but they wouldn't tell this to just anybody. In fact, they have only told each other, though only in their heads, only in thought. Yes, they stood in an invisible circle and had a long discussion about the pulsation, how despite their very brief connection to the egg, this beat has become their heartbeat. It is true that these people, all men of course, stood in an invisible circle and placed one hand on their hearts and one hand on the imaginary heart of the man directly to his right, and so on and so forth, and it is true—they felt unification. They touched only for a minute and then they went on with their lives. They have never spoken about this moment, and it's quite certain they never will, unless of course, they were to meet again, but this is unlikely because at least two of the men have passed. It's said that at the time of their death, the men who were still living felt their hearts implode for a full minute, then their hearts began beating at the exact pace as before, neither missing nor skipping beats, even though for that prior full minute, they had been certain they would die. And inside that red freckled egg, something magical happened.

Still, we watch the egg, carefully noting the men who come up to it, touch it quickly and retreat. We hope one of these men will be the man to bring about the change, that one of these men will be special. The egg is waiting for someone, and when he arrives, maybe, just maybe, this red freckled egg will hatch.

The Poets

Unlike storytellers, who had a utilitarian function, poets weren't very useful. It was the poets' duty, their task and purpose, to retain the stories of the past in the various cavities of their bodies. Poets were created with many empty sacs. Rather than real livers or lungs, they survived on the memory of those organs. Their bodies were essentially empty pockets, a hollow skeleton holding up skin.

The poets stored the past in these pockets. They were the primary method of historical preservation. As such, poets were a required presence at all major meetings of any important Council, and it was common practice for wealthy families to retain their own personal poet.

Although this description makes poets sound useful—even integral—to society, they were often unreliable. They regularly misconstrued facts for the joy of it. Because poets understood they were necessary commodities, they abused their abilities of translation, and when asked about certain events or words, they offered skewed recollections.

We have tried to ask the storytellers to help us decipher truth from fiction, but poets and storytellers have the same memory, the same fate, and we can't trust what either of them say.

Betty's Abbreviated Life

Mama Sylph is an ordinary woman. She's a little robust, and the men love it. Before she was Mama Sylph, she was Betty.

Betty did not do an abnormal thing her entire life. Growing up, she lived in a white two-story house with a white picket fence. She had two brothers and a little poodle named Daisy. Her mama and papa were good, hard-working people, and they ate dinner at six o'clock sharp every night, and every night at dinner, they'd talk about their day. In high school, Betty was a cheerleader, but don't get the wrong idea. She was also in band (she played the flute) and she was an honor student. She was president of her class. People loved her. When Betty went to college, she was a proud member of the Tri Delta sorority. She majored in English and met the love her life, Stanley Sylph. Except he wasn't really the love of her life. He was just a guy she let into her bed. Before she knew it, she was pregnant and then she wasn't Betty anymore, she was Mrs. Sylph. Then, she wasn't even Mrs. Sylph anymore but Mama Sylph.

The day she gave birth to the Sylph boys, Mama Sylph didn't think they would be attached. No one did. The doctors hadn't even told her to expect twins, but still, out they came. Oddly enough, Stanley Sylph had two perfect names picked out for the connected boys, almost as if he knew they were on their way.

The Extinction of Poets and Philosophers

There was a time when all men lived in water. Back then, there were more than ten species of humans, some of whom have survived, such as men, mermen, and arguably, prophets and storytellers. Many others have gone extinct. Poets and philosophers were the first to die, their lungs unable to withstand the gravitational weight as they emerged from the deep ocean. They were delicate creatures and not particularly smart. They were much akin to goats or sheep. They would follow each other, without a clear leader, huddling in packs, pushing each other forward. It was the force of that push that allowed any movement at all. If a poet was pushed westward, the whole pack would follow.

These species of man were particularly vulnerable to bruises and skin breaks. Often, a poet or philosopher would cut his own skin and let his blood lead the pack, and they, faithful followers, would shimmy around the water, meandering behind the blood, until the blood, being thicker than water, floated upwards and upwards, until their skin sank into the muscles, diving deeply into their own pores. Then, the muscles dissolved into the bones until even the bones had nowhere left to go. Eventually, the bones floated to the surface of the water, and the surviving poets and philosophers followed and followed until nothing remained of them except a large number of free floating bones.

Prophets

As a species, prophets were much like storytellers. They didn't have a specific body type to distinguish them from other species, but unlike storytellers, who were photocopies or clones, prophets would find a body they liked and imagine death until the body's life was removed, and the prophet would slip into the vacated carcass. Much like storytellers, it is assumed that prophets have been extinct for many centuries and eons, but this cannot be substantiated because they are body nomads.

According to the rumors of man, prophets were very cruel. He'd kill another body before there was any malfunction in the body he'd just acquired. To maintain strength and to ensure there would be no questions or strings, it was typical for prophets to eat the body left behind. Depending on the species he chose to live in, it could be quite difficult to consume another body. Man, for instance, is only accustomed to moon vegetation; flesh of any kind could make her quite ill, but the prophets don't care. They imagine the body can chew through bone and the body does. Prophets are frightening. Long before prophets went extinct, all the other species petitioned the Extinction Sub-Committee of the Evolution Council to ask that prophets, as a species, be removed from earth. Prophets, upon hearing this rumor through their man-spies, began to concentrate on extinguishing the Extinction Sub-Committee, and that was the end of the Extinction Sub-Committee. Unfortunately, they had forgotten to destroy the petition itself, and the remaining Evolution Council, upset at the great loss of their fellow Council members, quickly signed it into law.

It's unclear if any prophets survived this cleansing, but it would not be at all surprising if many of them simply disguised themselves, making their prophetic nature invisible in order to survive. It wouldn't be the first time prophets were forced to disappear.

Before the last, or seemingly last, prophet was killed, he was said to have said that there would be a great revolution based on evolution, that the Councils will be to blame, if only in part, and there would be a clash of species, and many would die. He gave the revolution a time, far into the future, so far away that although many ignored his words, they saw the way he crunched his eyelids down so hard a small crack appeared on the ridge of his nose. Those who were there claimed that he cemented the future right there, right before his death. This last prophet decided to destroy the earth, just like that.

Birthday

She is sure her mother was a prophet and knowing of her ensuing death, as a prophet would, she passed her legacy down to her daughter. Chloe Henklemeyer doesn't know much about her mother, but she's been told her mother spoke only one word before dying. She's been told the one word she spoke was "Chloe," and the nurses assumed it was her intention to name her baby Chloe. They took her mother's last word to be a sign, and as Susan, the assistant to the head nurse, gently blew the black ink dry on the very white birth certificate, she realized that Chloe's mother's name was also Chloe. Susan, assistant nurse to the head nurse, realized this small misunderstanding and ran back into the room with the other nurses, the dead Chloe, and the very much alive baby Chloe, to explain the whole situation. The nurses conferred and decided it would be best to leave the child's name as it was, as a token, a remembrance, of her lost mother.

Later that night, the assistant nurse, Susan, who was a very nice lady, walked out of the hospital after working a twelve-hour shift with baby Chloe in her backpack. She walked slowly and evenly, so to not attract attention from too many people. As she walked, she hummed a soft tune to keep Chloe from crying, but Chloe wouldn't have cried anyway. She had just inherited a mother, a prophet.

The story of Chloe's birth changes every year. One year, Susan told her a version where her father, an arrogant prince of a man, walked into the hospital room just in time to hear her mother whisper the name Chloe, and he, being a prince thereby practically a fairy tale, strode over to her and said, "Not yet my love," and her mother, having always been a sucker for fairy tales, woke up with a cough, and the three of them lived happily ever after.

Another year, Chloe made up her own version of events where she wasn't given up for adoption and the family that took her in didn't make her cobble shoes all day. In this version, she wears clothes like Cinderella, but there isn't a prince. In Chloe's versions, there are never any princes. Sometimes, she'll include a toad, but when she kisses it, she inevitably gets boils that can't be cured.

Every year, Susan and Chloe create a new story for her birth, and for that entire year, whatever story they derive becomes fact, but only for that year, only until her next birthday arrives. For this mother-daughter pair, Chloe's birthday is the best day of the year.

The First Story

When she was a small girl, but long before she'd wanted spectacles to decorate her face, long before she was even a girl baby—this, in fact, occurred in the days directly before she was born, just days before her mother left her—she heard her very first story.

If you ask her, she will tell you she remembers the story exactly as her mother said it, every word in its proper place, exactly as her grandmother had told her mother, exactly how her great-grandmother had told her grandmother when she was still in the womb and so on and so forth. But if you ask her to relay this sacred story passed down by generations of mothers to their female bellies, just to verify that there was indeed a story and perhaps even the same story, she won't tell you. If you ask her to tell this great tale, even if you ask politely, she will shake her head nimbly. She will divert her eyes down to the tip of her pointed nose until you ask again and again, and each time you ask, her eyes will wander a little deeper into the pores of her nose, and when you've exhausted yourself, begging her to tell you this story that you don't even care about any more, she'll turn around and leave.

A New Baby Boy

Stanley was born a single boy, but when he was in his Mama Sylph's belly, he had a twin sister. The doctors didn't know about them being attached, but his mama did. Mama Sylph picked out the name Sylvia for her. She loved the idea of twin babies, attached by a small piece of skin, little wrinkled blobs of baby attached like friends. It was her idea, them being attached like that, but Stanley didn't like the idea of a sister so he made her disappear.

Sometime along the twenty-ninth week, fetus Sylvia disappeared from his mama's belly. Mama Sylph was at the doctor's office getting a sonogram. Both babies were there. They were holding their small hands. The doctor swore he saw Stanley gently rubbing Sylvia's hand, soothing her, and then, just like that, Sylvia disappeared. No heart beat, no remains, nothing.

It wasn't uncommon for fetuses to be miscarried, especially with a tentative pregnancy like Mrs. Sylph's, fragile twins and all, but the doctor had never seen anything like this. There had to be remnants somewhere, bits of baby floating in Mrs. Sylph's body somewhere, but there was nothing. There was nothing anywhere, almost as if Sylvia had never existed at all, almost as if someone had gone in and erased her from the manuscript, only it was more than just erasure. You can see the imprint of remains after erasure. No, it was more like someone just hit the delete key while typing Sylvia.

The doctor didn't tell Mrs. Sylph about this sudden change in her body. He thought maybe it was in his own head, but later that night, he went over her file, and in all the other sonograms, there's another small, distinct body. Up until she gave birth, Mrs. Sylph expected to have conjoined twins, and when just one small wrinkled glob of baby came out instead of two, and after it smashed its eyes and cried, suddenly, no one remembered he should have had a sister. Even the pictures forgot.

The Spreading of the Word

Word spread quickly that she had fallen into the water. Man by nature enjoys juicy news, and she did not hesitate to elaborate fantasies as to how it had happened. Before the sun could be seen through the other side of the planet, the story of her fall was so distorted that the merman no longer existed. One man's version of the story went like this: "Emily was flying around as she was always flying around, you know, kind of crooked because she was a crooked kind of girl when a whole herd of rhinoceroses came charging at her and punctured one of her wings."

One man interjected, "What the hell is a rhinoceros?"

The storytelling man said, "It's a large bird with a horn the size of your arm."

The storytelling man said, "Emily was so scared, flying with one of her wings hurt, that she thought maybe she could take refuge on the surface of the water, poor girl. Without her eyes to tell her that the water wasn't solid, she couldn't know. How could she know? Poor girl."

The storytelling man was old enough to remember the day when man had eyes. She rarely mentioned it, but this was a desperate time. A man had just gone missing. For all she knew, the girl could be dead. For all she hoped, the girl was probably hurt pretty bad, probably would never fly again so she may as well be dead, but she hoped for the hurt. It made for much better stories.

Every man's story was slightly different. In another version, some man was jealous of another man so she gouged out her eyes and tore part of her wing, only to realize the man damaged was Emily, which was not the man she'd intended to harm. In another version, Emily picked a fight with a small pack of birds, thinking they were bees. She'd been craving honey, being pregnant and all. The birds pecked ferociously, creating holes in her skin and planting mites. The mites ate at her bone until she had no more bone. Luckily, the mites had damaged her nerves so she couldn't even feel the heights from which she fell.

Either way, the story of Emily's fall became renowned, and in every version, there was some mistake by some man because of their lack of eyes.

Within days of Emily's disappearance, the Imperial Council held a public forum to discuss the future of man. Men were becoming increasingly fearful. This was the first disappearance in a century. Men were most frightened because they'd heard stories about other men who lived in the water, how vicious they were, how they ate the carcasses of decomposed men from above the water, how they could both see and sing. The Imperial Council met and discussed options for man's vision. Days later, the Council had still not reached a decision. Months later, they remained deadlocked. Years later, when men had forgotten all about Emily, the Imperial Council decided that they should stay exactly as they were. They should not open their eyes, they should not look for Emily, for after all, it had been years, and everyone knew Emily was only a fable, a fairy tale. The Imperial Council, after such a long deliberation, had forgotten why they had even started discussing using their cemented eyes again.

Of course, news of their decision spread quickly around the skies of the earth.

Merman's Dream

Emily is caught in a merman's dream. Emily doesn't know how long she's been caught in this merman's dream, but the silence is overwhelming. Once, she tried to sing, to comfort herself, but her voice came out as soft cashmere.

In this merman's dream, Emily can feel desperation, but she's afraid it is her own desperation leaking into his dream. She knows if she can't interpret his dream, she can't escape. Emily doesn't remember falling into the ocean, but she does remember her life before the fall.

Then, out of nowhere, she hears him singing. His dream is a muted song and Emily uses her fingers to draw out the lyrics, which she must translate into Man, and when she has, she will be able to talk to the merman. Emily is sure that when she speaks to the merman, she will be able to convince him to free her.

Emily doesn't know about the merman's vengeful nature. She doesn't know that the merman isn't dreaming at all, that he's letting her think he's dreaming so she can waste the little breath she has left in interpretation. This merman is evil. He has no problem killing little angels, watching her little wings flipping slick in the water, and he laughs broadly. Emily hears this. She thinks it's another clue to help in her escape. Every movement, every change, is a path back up to the sky.

Dirt or Grass

After walking for a few minutes on the dirt path, Sylvester thinks that no, he much prefers the grass. He thinks it may be decades before he will walk on grass again, and before he can even weigh the positive attributes of dirt, sprouts of grass cushion his stride.

Grass

Sylvester Sylph doesn't rush his way through the maze. He walks deliberately, letting his step sink into the bright grass. He can't see the brightness, but dead grass doesn't feel like this. Of course, Sylvester can't really remember the last time he'd stepped on real live grass. His parents rarely let him and his brother outside. They didn't want to scare the neighbors. When the boys did go out, they were quickly escorted from the car to the tent. The head carnie and Mama Sylph didn't want to give viewers a sneak preview of the goods. Sylvester doesn't know why he still thinks of his mama in terms of his parents plural. Papa Sylph has been dead for years, and the Sylph boys have been in the carnival circuit for five times as many years as their papa's been dead.

So Sylvester takes his time walking. He knows if he gets to the egg, this will be over and he'll be half of a two-headed boy again, but as long as he's caught in this labyrinth, he can be a single boy with single thoughts and singular happiness. He takes a step and the grass springs coils against his feet.

A Caveat

We cannot be held responsible if some of these events are not quite in order, if some of the facts are slightly out of place. We did not live through this, and what few facts we do have are difficult to verify.

We have tried our best to make this clear and simple. We have tried very hard to reconstruct this history as it happened, but it's impossible to do so without some errors so we apologize in advance, before it becomes too murky. We have tried, and while we hope trying is enough, we're afraid it isn't, that the inevitability of the future is already set, that maybe the prophet wasn't talking about the Evolutionary Revolution, that maybe the prophet was talking about something we can stop, if only we can get things right. We are trying. We're trying very hard, but we can't do it all on our own, if only we could have help, if only we could get you involved. We're weak and few in number, but that does not mean we do not try, lord only knows, it does not mean we do not continue trying.

Beautiful Sylvia

Everyone loves Sylvia Sylph. Even people who have never met her. Her mama thinks it's her eyes. Mama Sylph always tells Sylvia, "Baby girl, it's those magic eyes of yours. You hypnotize people when you look at them. It's a magic power, baby girl. Don't use it for bad. You're beautiful, and beauty is powerful. People will follow you so be careful, my baby girl. Be careful."

Mama Sylph gives Sylvia this speech, word for word, on the first day of every month of every year of her life. Still, Sylvia never listens to her mama. What teenage girl would? Especially a beautiful one!

Sylvia Sylph has boyfriends, lots of them. None of them have another boy attached to them. This is something Sylvia notices but has only mentioned once. Once, when she was kissing her very first boyfriend, a boy she trusted so much her skin tingled, she asked if he had a conjoined twin at home somewhere. He never talked to her again. Oh, he tried to spread nasty rumors about her too, but Sylvia has that special smile that stops movement. This first boyfriend, he disappeared on the very same day he tried to say terrible things about Sylvia Sylph. She didn't miss him. She cried a little the next day when the principal came over the intercom to tell the whole school he'd been lost, but the second Sylvia started to cry, the whole school gathered to pull the tears away from her face. They grabbed at her face earnestly, eagerly trying to help her. She looked at them, still a little devastated, and they shoved her tears into their own eyes until she had no more sadness left in her at all.

Eliot Comes Home

By the time Eliot Sylph reached his front door, the sun had nearly risen. It was still at that aching neon stage, and Eliot was sure there were still drums beating hard, using his various ribs to distill tone and cadence. Eliot knew he needed to slow down before walking into the house. He knew Sylvia would be able to detect an abnormality almost instantaneously. As Eliot Sylph stood outside his suburban home, he wondered why Sylvia hadn't told on him yet, but he quickly repressed the thought. Instead, he thought about how his darling little sister, so pretty and sweet, would never use her powers to tattle without some sort of provocation.

Outside his suburban home this early in the morning, he looked like any other normal teenager who'd stayed out too late, sneaking back into his house, hoping not to wake his parents, but this wasn't the case with Eliot Sylph. He wasn't afraid of waking his mama. His mama wasn't a problem at all. If anything, she was a pushover, a drunk. She was practically a whore, he thought. He laughed, thinking of how Sylvia would be laughing at this thought. He could almost hear her shrill giggle. It was becoming of her, that giggle.

He continued laughing for a few more seconds, thinking he'd calmed Sylvia down after he'd thought that nasty thought of her tattling on him or doing something else mean. He didn't want to think of her that way, but more importantly, he didn't want her to think he thought of her that way because everyone knows mermen will go to any length to enact revenge.

Sylvester Enjoys his Walk

Sylvester wishes he could be here for the rest of his life, forever a single boy who isn't afraid of being outside. Sylvester moves slowly. He's savoring, but he's still propelled forward. This is not in his control. He doesn't exactly know where he is headed or what makes him move in a particular direction, and he's OK with this. He's doing what he's supposed to do to stay in this world, and if he doesn't play along, he'll go back to the real world, a world of modern men and women, where he and Eliot are relics to be prodded with curiosity.

He knows this isn't Sylvia's doing, but he can tell that she's near, that she's watching to make sure he's alright. This makes him grin. He wonders if she can feel the grass under his feet and if she appreciates it the way he does.

This is a sacred time for him, the first real time he's been a single boy, so he has to make himself slow down to enjoy all the precious, minute details of this dreamscape. It's really very intricate, he thinks.

"Hey Sylvester," he hears.

"Just a little bit longer," he begs.

"OK, Sly, but just five more minutes."

Eliot's voice is soft, muted, but Sylvester is used to this kind of sound in his dreams. He's trained his ears to hear for just such an occasion.

Moving Day

It's true the Sylph boys didn't leave the house often, except when the carnival came to town, but that was just to make a little extra money for the family. Mama Sylph wasn't cold or uncaring, displaying her boys like freaks for people to touch in amazement. She was practical. It isn't cheap, buying clothes for two-headed boys, especially the way they were connected. For a while, the government helped the Sylphs. They gave them money for food and clothes, but then, the people in their picket fence neighborhood started to throw rocks into their windows, so the Sylphs had to move to a different place, a place where no one knew the boys.

Everyone knew their little sister Sylvia though. She was stellar hot.

The day the Sylphs moved from their picket fence neighborhood in the town they'd always lived, Papa Sylph was sad. The Sylph boys don't remember this, but Mama Sylph does, and she never talks about it. The day they moved away, Papa Sylph carried each and every box to the moving van, never letting his boys or his wife lift even the smallest container. Sylvia hadn't been born yet. She was in fact at this point only a forethought in her mama's fallopian tube.

After Papa Sylph packed the very last box into the van, he kissed his wife with sympathy, gave both his boys a hug and a high five and tussled their hair, and even rubbed his wife's belly, just for good luck, and then Papa Sylph walked into the house one last time. He walked through every room, snapshotting memories that hadn't yet been created. Then, he went into the bathroom, took a leak, and injected a syringe full of air into his veins.

Mama Sylph didn't cry that day, that day they moved away, but she swears she felt a new heart beating next to hers, a smaller, fainter heart, and she knew she would name her baby Sylvia, her husband's favorite name.

Of course, Mama Sylph had no way of knowing her husband once had a twin sister, a conjoined twin sister named Sylvia, but we think the fetus, little fetus Sylvia still in her mama's fallopian tubes, did. We think she knew it all along.

A Rumor, Dispelled

The sea has not become any more or less salty since that one decisive moment. We would like to think differently, that eventually, we can actually correct the mistakes someone else made at some other point in time, but we can't. This is the state of things. We must accept it. The sea is full of salt, and it will remain so until we can invent a mechanism to remove it, but even then, the mermen will make sure the memory of salt remains, if only as an afterthought, if only as a final act of revenge.

Stanley Sylph Makes an Enemy

Stanley Sylph was a good man. No one would ever think of saying a bad thing about him, except, of course, that he abandoned his family. No one disliked him, but everyone would have agreed the only thing Stanley Sylph ever did wrong was his last act, his legacy, his suicide. Everyone would agree his suicide was a cowardly act, a pathetic act enacted by a cowardly, pathetic man. So despite his affability, he is tainted by the one act in his life he had no control over. Indeed, Stanley Sylph was a controlled man up until that final moment when he walked into the house for the last time. Then, something changed. Something must've changed.

We want to believe Stanley Sylph didn't want to do it. We want to think he's a stronger man than that, but we can't. We can't because his suicide was planned. He knew he would die by his own hand before he walked back into the house, that this head tussle and that hug would be his final tussles and hugs, that he would never experience another high five, that he would never kiss his wife again. It must've been a hard moment, that moment of final good-bye.

We mourn the way he died, not that he died with a syringe in his arm, but the way it happened. We pity him. And he must've pitied himself because he prepared his own needle full of air, because he hid it in the cupboard above the stove, because he knew Betty wouldn't bother to check up there, because she was too lazy to use a ladder. We pity the day he went to go buy that syringe. Or maybe he stole it. That would be much more pathetic. We like Stanley Sylph as a pathetic man. It's easier to kick him now that he's dead, and we like easy things. Yes, he must've stolen the syringe, being so desperate and not wanting anyone else to know of his final choice. We think he stole it from someone even more pathetic than him, a homeless man, a drug addict.

But no, this is too much. Stanley Sylph was a good man, and we cannot disgrace his legacy anymore. None of this is true, although we want it to be. We want to remember Stanley Sylph as a weak man who abandoned his family, but the truth of it is that he had no control over what he was doing. Someone manipulated him, someone very small, barely even alive inside Betty's unprotruding belly. We want to think Stanley Sylph committed suicide because that's much more palatable than acknowledging that our darling Sylvia could have killed her own father. But that's the truth. If you asked her, she'd look at you blankly. She'd say nothing. But the truth is she didn't like him, her own father. She was the only person who's ever disliked Stanley Sylph, and this made her dislike—no, hate—him even more.

And poor Stanley, he had no idea Sylvia even existed. He should have. He should've felt her immediately, but he was preoccupied with leaving his childhood home and he was worried about his boys. He tried, lord knows he tried, to make people love his boys, but there were too many of them and their minds were too closed to embrace difference, and his boys, they would never be accepted. Yes, he should have felt his daughter hatch, but in his head, Stanley Sylph kept imagining his boys—his boys with one body and two heads—on a rotating stage, people prodding them to make sure they're really connected, and the day two strong men, one on each boy, would pull and the skin would divide, and there would be pain, so much pain. Stanley Sylph was focused on too many other things to account for his behavior, so when he stole the syringe from the homeless man, he didn't even know it happened, and when he tussled his boys' heads for the last time, he did it haphazardly, but when he touched his wife's belly, the last time he'd ever touch her skin, he felt the heartbeat. But by then, it was too late. It was inevitable, because by then he was already as good as dead.

The Proposal

Years before the Evolutionary Revolution, mermen decided unanimously to divide themselves in half, to single themselves from double-headed form to single-headed form. It is rare that mermen decide on anything, much less in agreement. The weight of this decision was further intensified as mermen had been double-headed forms since their creation, but still, they came up with their unanimous decision only moments before the final proposals for evolution were due to be reviewed and either accepted or denied by the Evolution Council. Given the rapidity of the agreement and the impending time deadline, they scarcely had time to negotiate the specific terms of separation. Their decision and proposal, so hastily made and drafted, full of mechanical errors and outright improper word choice, was not something that would easily pass the Evolution Council. So they rapidly forgot that they had requested a bodily change. Mermen were not only forgetful beings, they were also drunks. The moment the proposal reached the Evolution Council, they began to drink, and they drank passionately, so passionately in fact that moments later they had forgotten their reason for celebration, they forgot everything.

It should be noted, however, that although they couldn't remember things as important as petitions to Evolution Councils, they never forgot any wrongdoing enacted upon them. Ever. Their lives were perpetual missions of revenge, for with every successful act of revenge, the merman being revenged would think the act unworthy or too worthy, thereby setting forth a whole new chain of revenges and so more revenge and more revenge and so on and so forth.

Emily, Resigning

Emily can't tell if she's in a merman's dream or if she is just underwater. Her senses are useless and she's sure she will die. Emily wishes man had asked for foresight as a sense, but she isn't even sure if that would help her now. Emily tries breathing, and it's difficult. She struggles for a few seconds, so that she can say she tried. She's cold. She thinks it's possible her skin has retreated behind her muscles. She considers the probability that even her muscles have hidden, that she is nothing but skeleton floating in either ocean or dream. It doesn't matter which one she is in; she's helpless either way.

Another Rumor, Dispelled

Contrary to popular belief, the mermen's building of walls made of bone did not cause the ocean to become salty. Nor did the fall of man cause the sea to become salty. Although these are related, one event did not cause another did not cause another. It is impossible to say whether one reaction could have spilled into another reaction which may have caused something else entirely unrelated. And no one can say for sure if any unrelated thing was the thing that made the sea salty, but whatever it was, the sea has remained salty ever since. Whatever it was, it must have contained a very concentrated amount of Sodium Chloride.

Storytellers' Function

The storytelling man tells us she is a storyteller, that she is the last of the great line of storytellers, but we don't believe her. She looks like any other man to us, and her stories just aren't that great. She tries to explain that it isn't the storyteller's function to tell a good story; rather, it is to create a story to verify the truth behind a statement or idea. Either the statement or idea is true or it isn't. It is the storyteller's function to distinguish the difference. In the days when the Evolution Council was strongest, so strong in fact that many worried the Council was misusing their power and authority, some men formed the Imperial Council in opposition and secretly met at the Golden Tree.

Unlike the Evolution Council, the Imperial Council consisted only of man, and these men were smart and fair, as all men are. The only other species allowed to sit during Council meetings were storytellers, who could not join the Council's discussion, except to verify truthfulness, and poets. Storytellers were devious, in a good-natured way. It was not uncommon for storytellers to morph into man form so to be more active participants in the discussions.

The storytelling man does not know why his kind went extinct, or if they were indeed extinct. She has tried using her storytelling abilities to decipher truth from dream, but having been in man's body for so long, she can't translate her own stories, getting lost between metaphors and character development. The storytelling man is trying though. She is trying to find another storyteller, a friend, someone who looks just different enough to help her find her story again.

The Golden Tree

Although it is called the Golden Tree, it's impossible to say if the tree was actually golden in tint or if it was made of solid gold. We don't even know if the tree had golden leaves. It is, however, known that the Imperial Council called it the Golden Tree, and as such, there must've been something gold in the tree, unless, of course, the Imperial Council wanted to throw everyone off track.

The tree is housed in a deep labyrinth inside the moon, somewhere near the very core of our dead satellite, our nightly companion, which is why we cannot substantiate the color or species of tree. Because the Imperial Council met there first in daydream, because they imagined the tree into reality, now that we are trying to slowly reconnect our past, now that we are trying to decipher truth from myth, we cannot.

It is not that we haven't tried. We have followed the myth, setting our bodies straight and flat and willed our minds to rest. We have written the scripts for our daydreams, instructing them to transport us to the center of the moon, to the Golden Tree. We have invoked our forefathers, citing ourselves as the descendants of the Imperial Council, but nothing has happened. They must've known we were false portrayals.

We are fearful that the day the moon went dry and dormant, the Golden Tree wilted and died like any other tree. We are worried the tree's center became hollowed with rot, and without the Golden Tree, how can decisions be made? Without the Golden Tree, how can the Imperial Council maintain equilibrium for the earth?

Yes, we are growing concerned. We are trying daily, attempting to make contact with the tree. We even sent men to the moon to find an opening in its surface that could lead into the labyrinth that we must navigate to find the tree. But we are losing hope. Every day, we lose just a small amount more, as if hope can flake off, like dry skin or bark.

Survival

Whatever it is inside the egg is growing. There are times when the freckles suddenly flare, exploding bursts of steam before receding back. We are reminded of volcanoes and geysers, but this is an egg, and we shouldn't let our minds wander too far from fact.

Sometimes, we hear a sound reminiscent of either a groan or a woodpecker. We watch the shell become flexible, and we see something push against the lush cashmere wrapping. The bulge created is too large to fit inside the egg. We wonder if maybe it is one of those magical houses. The ones where the exterior is small but once you step inside, it magnifies. We wonder if maybe there is something huge inside, something that is larger than anything we have ever seen before, maybe a dinosaur or a dragon. We're sure whatever it is doesn't belong. It is a relic. We know that in every generation, a relic from another time comes to live among us. We're not sure how it happens, but the relic always appears. And we keep our eyes open for these things. It is what we do. We must try to keep it together. It is our only chance of survival.

This egg would not survive if it weren't for us. It is our duty to maintain life, no matter how horrible that life may be.

The Imperial Council

Since its formation, the Imperial Council has met at the Golden Tree. Located in the center of the moon, the tree is difficult to see, but this was the Council's desire. They needed a secluded venue to discuss man's future as a species and of course, a secret place, an impenetrable place, to talk about the ways they could ensure global domination. Because of this tender topic, the Council created the Golden Tree at their first meeting and agreed to meet there twice a year at a designated time. And so it went.

Of course the other species suspected these meetings, but they couldn't be proven. The Imperial Council, to maintain appearances, continued to meet publicly, with both official poets and storytellers present, but these meetings were merely fronts. Nothing of any importance was ever discussed during these public meetings. Most often, the meetings never went beyond the reading of the previous meeting's minutes. To occupy time, the Council members would dispassionately debate this or that small detail, improper wording, specific miscalculations, until their designated time for this particular meeting expired and nothing of any substance was discussed. The next meeting, they would rehash the minutes from the previous meeting, which was nothing more than a rehash of the previous meeting's minutes, which certainly was another prolonged argument about the previous meeting's minutes, and so on and so forth.

According to several poets' accounts, the original meeting's minutes, which were always discussed, had never even happened, or at least, they had no memory of it. According to several storytellers, the entire meeting was a fiction, every single part of it.

Rejoining Ritual

After he waits for a full five minutes, Eliot Sylph lies down next to his brother's head. He carefully adjusts their necks and uses bits of discarded hair and mucous to sew them back together. Then, Eliot wills himself to sleep.

The change is instantaneous.

Even in sleep, his body struggles. Sylvester is trying to stay in his dream; he doesn't want to give it up yet. He's sure his brother feels that same lack of flexibility, that immediate elimination of freedom.

There in his dream, Eliot wishes he would wake up and be a single boy again. But that isn't possible. Instead, he knows when they wake up, they'll once again be *The Amazingly Connected Sylph Boys! Come and touch 'em if you don't think they're real!* Eliot hates it when people touch him. Especially strangers. Especially strangers who are single people. He hates them most. Especially if they're beautiful.

Eliot knows Sylvester had begged for more time, that Sylvester loved being in that maze, wherever it was. Eliot wishes he could always be a single boy. He isn't content being a double boy, a carnival freak.

Eliot feels a hand slap his face, and he can hear Sylvester scream back to reality.

Our First Storyteller

We aren't sure what's inside the egg, but we have heard the stories the storytellers have told in response to our own stories, and we have listened carefully. Storytellers are coy, and we must give them our full attention, lest we miss an integral word here or there and the whole story has changed meaning. It is easy to understand why the storytellers have been so marginalized. In truth, we do not like them. We would prefer them to leave us alone, but it is our responsibility to protect them, all of them who have come from past times. We must ensure their survival so they can be studied and understood.

But these storytellers, they are a particular nuisance. They are difficult to look at when they look just as we do, when they contort their bodies to mirror our own. We cannot discipline a face with our same nuances, and their stories, they are often boring, but we know we must listen, and so we pay attention in shifts, and later, as a whole, we convene to share notes. But this is an inefficient system. We know we must all listen, we must all take notes, and even then, we must convene to compare what we have heard, but it is impossible for us to be so attentive for months at a time. They are full of words, these storytellers. Often, we think they use so many words out of malice. When we feel this way, we challenge them to leave, but they never do. They promise to behave.

When we acquired our first storyteller, we did not believe he was a true storyteller. We were sure the storytellers had been extinct for eons, but we also knew of their cunning ways. Obviously, we tested him. We made several statements, and he spoke to each one. Then, we were sure. He was a storyteller. Later, when we convened to discuss his future, if he should be with us, a part of us or apart from us, we learned that each of us heard a slightly different version of the stories he'd told. He'd spoken to all of us at once, and somehow, we heard different words. It is unlike us to disagree like this; we have phonographic memories and could recount his stories verbatim, and as certain as the moon was once arable, each of us heard a variation of the same tale. Every version brought the same result, the same indictment of fact or fiction, and because the storyteller still functioned as storytellers ought to, we were forced to keep him, often against his will. With us. For safekeeping, for protection.

And again, we have forgotten about the egg. Soon though. Soon, it will hatch, and we will see what lurks beneath all that cashmere.

How the Sea Became Salty

The day the word came from the Evolution Council that the mermen could not divide their two-headed forms into one-headed forms, the mermen were angry. They made a pact to stop drinking, to maintain focus. Given their predisposition to forgetfulness—they had entirely forgotten their desire to separate along with the petition outlining their request—they resolved to organize as a coalition to protest the Council's decision. The mermen, in fact, took the decision as an act of aggression against them as a species. They had heard rumors about how other species were allowed great variations in evolution, and so the fact that they had been denied was simply unacceptable.

But we digress. Let us suffice to say that the mermen eventually separated, and after separation, they had no idea how to negotiate life. After a decade or so of perpetual war, they built walls out of algae, only to learn that algae is permeable. So they erected barricades of coral, only to learn that coral crumbles with a merman's deep exhale. So they did the unthinkable. They began to kill fish indiscriminately. They ate the small fishheart, pulled out all the small fishbones, and discarded the remainder of the carcass. They built their walls out of bones, crocheting intricate doilies that could not be passed. They built them so high that they broke the surface of the ocean. Man flying in the atmosphere watched, eagerly gossiping, as mermen reached their hands into the air weaving bone into fabric.

But we digress. Let us suffice to say that there was once a time when mermen lived in clean water and man flew in the clean atmosphere, and one day, this order was disturbed and that was the day the sea became salty.

The Birthing of Mermen

Mermen are birthed, this much is true, but they do not have mothers and fathers. Mermen, when they are born, use their fisted feet to kick through insulating cashmere, through their weathered, leathery shell, to feel the rush of the cool ocean on their soft skin. When they feel this, they immediately want to retreat back into their shell, their womb. They quickly contort their bodies, flipping circles around their brothers, back to their egg, but it is too late, and with every movement, their egg disintegrates just a little bit more. These young mermen don't understand notions of cause and effect, so they continue their hectic movements until the remnants of egg are torn into bite-sized pieces. Now, hungry from exercise and desperation, they eat greedily, these baby mermen eat without notions of cause and effect, they eat until they have forgotten the egg entirely, until they have no recognition of where they came from.

This is the case for all mermen. This unified reaction is something bred into them by the Evolution Council. Mermen are born naturally greedy.

Mermen are birthed, this much is true, but they do not have mothers and fathers. Mermen are created in an artistic act. Connected merbrothers carefully remove pieces of themselves, parts of the body integral to survival, each brother giving up only what the other has so that between the two of them, they can still live, less strong but still living, one giving up a pancreas, the other an arm, until there are only enough parts for a full merman. The brothers then knead their discarded parts with a sharp whirling motion. They move it quickly, evenly, like a lump of clay on a potter's wheel, and when they are satisfied, they catapult this rotating thing into the ocean. As this merfetus spins, the ocean cocoons it in thick mucous. Eventually, the wrapped merfetus drops downward, down to the middle of the ocean, where coldness chills a shell and the mucous transforms into a cashmere placenta. Inside, little mermen form and continue to spin, never knowing who made them, even though they are all connected, even though they were not created from blood but from body, all of this will be forgotten for revenge, for self.

The Ed Brothers, Part I

Edmund and Edward have always hated each other. Ever since they were merboys, they've wanted separation. Edmund and Edward, by the time they broke through their cashmere wrapping to kick open the hard shell, they were the equivalent of ten years old, human time. Mermen are hatched fully developed.

By all accounts, the Eds were quite late. Most mermen leave their eggs in half the time, but because the Eds were so contrary, it took them much longer than expected. Their father had long abandoned them, and so when they finally emerged, they were alone and floating in the middle of the ocean, unable to breathe, unable to use their fins in tandem, and as the other mermen watched, they were sure the Eds would drown to death. The other mermen had never seen such contrary brothers before. They'd never seen such fierce desires for revenge develop so quickly; nor had they ever seen such forgiveness.

The other mermen quickly discussed whether or not to help these newborn merboys or to let them die. They were sure these boys would be trouble, that nothing good could come from them, but they couldn't let them drown. One merman extended a hand, which Edward grabbed and Edmund bit. Another merman slit temporary gills into their sides. The Eds stopped struggling so fiercely, and slowly, they collected their minds to wave their fins in tandem, and they swam away, very thankful.

The Ed Brothers, Part II

It's true that mermen, by nature, are cruel, but some mermen overcome this obvious defect, like a stutter.

Unfortunately for Emily, her merman was one who saw cruelty as a positive trait, something to be flaunted and adored. Fortunately for Emily, his best friend, who's also his brother, who's also attached to him, disagrees, and it was his song, this other brother's song, that Emily actually heard. This other brother had noticed Emily for years.

But unfortunately for Emily, the bad brother, Edmund the Worse, captured her in his dream and had no intention of freeing her. Edmund the Worse, in fact, enjoyed the fact that his weak, pathetic brother liked this man. He grinned to think his brother was worried about her so he catapulted her deeper into soundlessness. Fortunately for Emily, Edward the Better can free her, if he could only figure out how. Certainly, there is a way, but he doesn't know it yet.

Emily is in a precarious situation. Either Edward will save her and she will be his underwater bride forever, or Edmund will cage her in his dream and she will die of resignation.

Storytellers and the Egg, Part I

The day after we acquired our first storyteller, we got another. The next day, another joined us, and we were certain that storytellers had a silent network, but it was nothing so complicated. They had, one by one, verified stories until they could find our location.

We were not concerned at first. Sure, we'd heard stories about storytellers, but when we asked them to verify their truths, they showed no signs of fact. We have discussed the possibility that the storytellers have been lying to us all along, that they were never even storytellers, perhaps they were prophets or mermen, but we cannot speak about this too loudly, lest they overhear us.

We are growing concerned. There are many storytellers and many stories being told, and the stories are increasingly complex, difficult to follow, and many of them lack plot and character. A few of the stories have no beginnings, while others last so long we are sure the initial tale ended months ago, long before the storyteller wanted to stop, so he simply began another story and then another, a collection of them loosely connected.

It is a rule that storytellers can only tell stories in response to other stories. But these species of storytellers, they seem to be immune to the rule. When asked, they tell us that they are simply responding to a story they'd heard a while back, but being so busy, so pre-occupied with their current story, they'd been unable to properly attend to it before. We are confused with all these stories and storytellers. We think they are an infestation, a cancer.

We have asked them. Sometimes, they answer in one word story-responses. Sometimes, they simply say, *True*, or *False*. We hardly find these words adequate stories. We think they must be poets, and poets aren't a sturdy species.

We are growing concerned about these storytellers because they are increasingly interested in our egg. They tell perpetual stories about it, none of which make sense, but with each story, they come closer and closer to it, each story teasing location. It is as if their stories are an elaborate game of Marco Polo, and we are growing concerned because this is how they found us. We are not hidden, but they found us, and if they can find us, they can find our salvation. And we are not sure we want to be saved.

Man Emerging

The day man emerged from water, the sky stormed big shards of lightning, but man was unafraid. It is unclear how man segued from water to air, if she, like dolphins or whales, began by breaking the surface of water for brief moments or if she simply flapped her little wings underwater, using them as propellers, until she was lifted out of the water, into the sky. Or perhaps she was more like a duck or swan, sitting on the surface with her feet maintaining equilibrium, until she became bored by the moisture slicking off her skin and so she took flight out of simple ennui. Or perhaps she used the bodies of other men like a ladder, climbing slowly upwards, until she could jump from such great heights and learn to flap her wings before falling deeply back into the water. The only thing we know for sure is that man must have worked in conjunction with other men to transition from water to air.

It was no secret that the long time rift between man and merman had become trying for both species. It was also no secret that man had petitioned the Evolution Council for permission to inhabit the sky, and although the Council denied their proposal, they told them that even the Evolution Council cannot prevent the unavoidable, and it was unavoidable that man would take to the sky. The Council offered man a loophole. Although they could not, for unmentionable reasons, approve the petition, they would not erase its possibility. The Council told man's representative if she could find a way to survive in the atmosphere, the Council would ratify the petition, but only after man could prove she could thrive there. The Evolution

Council knew, even then, even at this very early stage of their existence, that they had no control, that they could not escape what prophets desired.

So the day man emerged from water, it stormed big shards of lightning, but every man had practiced flight. Every man knew how to breathe the atmosphere, how to close her eyes once she broke the surface of water. Every man knew she had to fly to survive, that she was on the verge of extermination if she stayed in the water. Of these men, it's said they were unafraid, but the stakes were high, and if they weren't scared, they must've been at least just a little bit nervous.

Storytellers & the Egg, Part II

We cannot be too lenient. There are now many storytellers among us. We think perhaps there are too many. We are afraid that soon, we will not be able to differentiate our bodies from their stories. We are afraid they have already infiltrated our task, our stories, and we are certain that some of their stories can be verified as truth and some cannot, but we can no longer tell the difference between the two. These chameleon storytellers, they are photocopies of ourselves, and we are already so variable, so expansive in number, we cannot trust anyone. We are afraid. We need leadership, someone to tell us what to do and who to believe. We are confused.

And our egg. It grows hotter and redder every day. Some days, its red is so intense it swallows all other color in its passion.

It must be hidden, our egg. It must be hidden even further away than it is hidden now. We are not conspiratorial. We are not being unreasonable. This is important, and we cannot be too lenient. We cannot be too trusting.

A Coincidence

It is a coincidence, we say. We are confident, most certainly positive, that this is a coincidence. The day Emily fell into the ocean so clean and pure, as pristine as an aquifer, was the very same day the mermen were told they could not be separated, that the Evolution Council declared they will forever remain two-headed mermen. But we are sure these things are unrelated.

Even though we know Emily's fate is not so very horrible, that she endured torture for only a limited amount of time, that all too soon, it will be over and she will be safe again, right now, right now we are in the midst of all that suffering, we feel like we too are swimming in smoldering cashmere. We feel like even thinking, even a small sigh, burns our poor, exhausted bodies.

But we know the Ed brothers did not lure Emily from the skies as a hostage, and that helps our suffering some. Knowing there is only one evil brother countered by one good brother, a coincidence in itself, this knowledge alleviates the remnants of heat we feel while retelling this story, and we are amazed at how deep and far Edmund's revenge can reach.

Emily in Panic

Emily does not care to breathe anymore. She tells her nostrils to constrict, but they do not listen. She reaches her fingers upward to clamp her nose shut only to find she doesn't have a nose. Where there should be a nose, there is a nub. It has no holes. Somehow, this doesn't surprise Emily. She isn't worried about how she will breathe, except she suddenly is worried. Before she'd thought about it, she was fine, but now she rubs the nub that was her nose abrasively, trying to dig nostrils, air passages, something. As her fingers claw deeper into this flesh that cannot be her own, she hears a voice, resentful in its depth, promising her torture. This voice booms explicit tales of suffering into her ears, which of course, are also gone, replaced by more little nubs.

When Emily calms herself enough to touch her new nubs with hope and kindness, qualities natural to man, she will hear her merman's song again.

This is something we know will happen once she calms herself, but she doesn't know this yet. She continues to grasp in panic, digging trails of blood, and Edmund's voice, rhapsodic in its terrors, keeps her hooked. Emily doesn't know that all she has to do is rely on her sense of kindness and everything will be OK. She doesn't know that Edward and his comforting song are waiting for her, waiting for her to breathe again.

Matrilineage

The mother had called her daughter on her twentieth birthday. When she didn't pick up the phone, the mother became worried and quickly rushed to her apartment. The daughter was just in the shower and hadn't heard the phone ring. Still partially wet but happy to see her mother, the daughter said, "Today, I woke up to find tiny wings on my legs, a pair on each side of my thighs."

The mother said, "They're not regular wings like you'd see on an angel. They're red and ugly, like they'd been hatched too early."

The daughter said, "I was scared to see them, they were so red and ugly I wished they weren't real. When that didn't work, and really, I didn't think it would, I tried to saw them off."

The mother said, "But first, you tried to pull them off."

The daughter responded, "Oh, that's good! That's absolutely right, I would've tried to pull them off first."

The mother said, "But then you were OK. Then you tried to make yourself fly."

"But I couldn't," said the daughter. The daughter said, "It's something I inherited from my mother who inherited it from her mother, but I have no proof because my mother's dead."

The mother said, "Not this mother, of course. Your real mother."

And the daughter laughed, "Of course not you, Mother. My real mother who died when she was twenty out of shock when she saw her red wings."

And the mother said, "Much like her mother had when she turned twenty, but not you, my daughter." She said, "You're different. You're so much stronger than your mothers. You can have your wings and your life."

And the daughter asked, "But what am I to do, Mother? What am I to do without the guidance and support of my mothers before me?"

Then the mother went away and the daughter finished drying herself off, eager for the year ahead. She looked down and saw her raw little red wings struggling to cut air.

The Truth about the Evolutionary Revolution

The truth is the Evolutionary Revolution was unplanned. It came about in a time of relative peace between man, merman, and all other beings. Yes, the Evolutionary Revolution was entirely unplanned, but just because it was unplanned does not mean it was unexpected. No, this revolution was something the Evolution Council had been expecting for centuries, but 'given that the revolution had been foretold more than ten centuries before it actually occurred, the Council assumed they had escaped the wrath of revolution. At least that's what they'd hoped. Still, there was always one small Council member who tried to remind the others about the coming of the revolution, that they should beware and prepare, but the Council members joked about the silly revolution. At every Council gathering, they joked, and at every Council meeting, that same small Council member reminded them how the last prophet foretold it, how the storytellers confirmed it, how they all knew what was at stake here. But the other Council members didn't listen. No, they just drank and laughed and guffawed, and the one member, he sulked in the corner, thinking how one day, they would understand, but by then, it would certainly be too late, at least that's what he hoped.

Of course, none of Council members, not even the one dissident voice, really understood what was at stake because prophets had been extinct for more than fifty centuries. It's not clear when the last of the storytellers went extinct. They were an amorphous species, changing bodies without difficulty. It is quite likely that a storyteller or two still exists today, but because no one is able to identify them as a species, they're just as good as extinct, and have been for a very long time now. So this myth of revolution has been passed down through the centuries through whispers, the most accurate and efficient delivery method, told by relics long since extinct. These rumors of impending revolution, now a full ten centuries late, didn't matter to the opulent Evolution Council.

So yes, the Evolutionary Revolution was unplanned, but it was so powerful, so life-altering, because it was, or should have been, expected.

The Sylph Boys Run in Bed

The Sylph boys are running in bed, legs mechanically extending and retracting, though neither boy controls the movement. The Sylph boys move synchronized, as if they were never divided, and as they fully wake, still running in bed, they are happy to see each other. They're happy because each boy can stop his motion individually. They're happy because this shouldn't be possible, but somehow, it is.

The Sylph boys are running in bed, only they're awake, and they're no longer connected. Each one has his own body and his own head, and each body and each head lays on his own separate bed, and suddenly, they wonder if they were ever connected at all.

A Daydream's Repercussions

The first meeting of the Imperial Council was held in a daydream.

Of course, back then, man lived underwater with all the other species of human, and because water was translucent and the sun's brightness never waned, every dream was a daydream, bright with anticipation and hope. It must have been the sunlight that tainted their dreams, giving their tree, their meeting place, a golden hue, and it must have been all that vivid light that made these men at this very first meeting decide that man should no longer live with other humans, that man should take to the atmosphere, and at night, to hide from the luminous brilliance of the sun, man should harvest a home on the moon.

Yes, the first meeting of the Imperial Council was held in a daydream, but much was accomplished at this first meeting, decisions were cast that would change the course of both mankind and the earth.

Later that day, although it was always day in the ocean, the Imperial Council announced the change, and men flapped their little red wings until water no longer blanketed their skin warm.

The Sylph Boys Laugh

They're no longer dreaming. This is real. The Sylph boys running in bed look at their individual legs, their four individual legs.

Sylvester says, "Eliot, stop running."

And Eliot stops.

And Sylvester keeps on going. Sylvester cycles his feet in the air, making a small whirlwind. It is visible, the way the air spins, like he is creating a time warp, a worm hole appearing right there, but both boys are too amazed with their individuality to notice.

Eliot says, "Stop moving your legs so that I can! Stop being so greedy!"

Sylvester says, "You went running just a few hours ago. You can wait."

Eliot says, "Well, you could've gone running too, but you decided to walk all slow."

Sylvester says, "Well, at least I didn't fall down. I knew how to walk without falling."

And Eliot says, "Asshole."

And they both laugh.

Their laugh is magnetic. It sends out waves of laughter. The Sylph boys chuckle, and it emanates, infecting people deep in their lungs, and these people, they start laughing too and as they laugh, they drift closer to the boys. People still asleep, some naked, some in two-piece pajamas, some drinking coffee, some in the middle of morning sex, they float towards the boys as they laugh, as their bodies fill with happiness.

When they stop, the floating bodies fall to the ground with a thump. People from all over the world wake, unaware of where they are and how they got there. It is unfortunate because many people were drifting over the ocean, and when they fell from the sky, they were not awake enough to swim. We can only hope mermen are not as vengeful as they once were.

An Army Inside an Egg

There are days when the egg radiates pure red and the heat is unbearable. When the egg shows signs of anger, we must divest our bodies of clothing. We sit in rivers, but the temperature rises so hot we fear the water may congeal or evaporate. We try to put as much distance between us and the egg, but always, someone keeps watch of the egg, someone brave enough to endure its wrath. When we return, our feet running swiftly on the scalding earth, he who kept watch, he is singed. He is steaming charcoal.

What we know about mermen we have heard only in story, but we are quite certain that the anger brewing inside the egg comes from more than just one or two mermen. It would not be possible for one being to be so angry. We would prefer not to think about the egg like this, but we have no option other than to believe that it is our duty, our reason for existence, to watch over a whole army of mermen maturing inside.

The Beginning of a Whole Year

When Chloe looks down at her little red wings, they are exactly as she described to her mother. She's a little surprised. She's surprised because she's never managed to change her physiology with a birthday story before, but this time, she's created little wings on her thighs, and she knows for this whole year, she'll have them, and suddenly, she regrets asking for them. She, in fact, has no idea how she got the idea of putting wings on her legs. It's the most ridiculous thing she's ever thought of, and she wonders why she would have declared this her fate for a whole year.

Chloe wonders if maybe she can change her fate, if maybe she can make them go away. So she rewrites the story. She says, "This is the year I'll fall in love. This is the year Susan and I will be separated forever because I'll fall in love. This year, I won't have red wings on my legs, but I will meet another freak, another person who was once two people but is now just one, and he'll be kind, and I won't fall in love with him, even though he's the one I'm supposed to love. No, I'll love his brother, and his sister will also love me, and Susan will finally stop calling. This is what will happen this year. I won't have little red wings attached to my legs. I won't."

And Chloe opens her eyes and expects the wings to have disappeared, but they haven't. She knows she only has one chance to write the future for the year, and that chance is gone. It has to be the first thing she and Susan come up with. It has to be their first story together. But Chloe doesn't like this story. She doesn't like the idea of being a freak, walking around with red wings stuffed deep in her jeans like she's got excess layers of fat rustling while she walks.

Chloe doesn't know how she'll work.   Chloe doesn't know how she'll even walk around. The wings trip over themselves, rub themselves rawer. She thinks maybe this will be the year she joins the carnival, traveling around, letting people touch her little wings. They like it, the wings, when they're touched. They nestle around fingers, chirping.   Chloe calls Susan, eager to tell her mother about her plans, and when the daughter announces her plans, the mother says, "Maybe we shouldn't speak this year," and the daughter says, "Why?" and the mother says, "I just don't think I can handle your future this year. I don't think I like the idea of you falling in love," and the daughter says, "I never said anything about falling in love."

Anger

Chloe has good reason to be upset with her mother, who now refuses to speak with her, who demands they not speak for the next year. Her mother, ranting, illogically screaming about the romanticization of love, her mother reminds her, as if Chloe needed reminding, that she's never aimed for love, never in her year-long adventures has she desired anything more than a mother-daughter bond. But now Chloe is twenty years old, and even Susan cannot expect her daughter to be only hers forever.

Happy Sylvia

Sylvia Sylph is happy because her brothers are single boys. Now she can live the life she wants because her mama can't keep her in a little genie bottle anymore, even though if she'd ever really wanted to, Sylvia could've released herself long ago. Sylvia knows she's special, that she can make anyone do anything she wants, but she still lets her mama control her. At least, she lets her mama think she controls her.

Sylvia's at that age when she thinks she knows everything, except the difference is she really does. If Sylvia wants to know anything, she can. Sylvia Sylph doesn't need Google or Ask Jeeves. She doesn't need search engines or the internet. Sylvia Sylph just closes her eyes, and her thoughts slink into some other person's head, and there, she gorges herself. Any information they have, she can have, and when she's in there, that person is completely vulnerable to her whims. When Sylvia wanders into another person's head, she can be lethal. Luckily, she's a nice girl and wouldn't do bad things, unless she thought that person really deserved it, unless that person had really done something really mean to her. Then, she would be forced to enact revenge, even though she's no merman. No, no one would be so silly as to imply that because she's obviously human, but there's a legacy inside her, a deep voice telling her she cannot let the wrongs of others go.

But she never feels this way with her brothers, especially now that they're single. Back when they were two-headed boys, she'd sometimes feel this way about her mama, but she never did anything about it. She was, after all, her mama. But now that her brothers are single boys, Sylvia feels free. Yet she can sense something different about her brothers, something she can't quite figure out. Sylvia can tell there's something else brewing, and when she tries to enter Sylvester's head, something very big and hot forces her out, something with a thick, steady beat. She's never had difficulty reading Sylvester. When she tries to go into Eliot's head, Sylvester stands in her way, his whole naked body filled with chicken pox. He looks at Sylvia, desperate, and says, "Help us."

Sylvia has never been afraid. She's never even been a little bit scared, but there in Eliot's head, looking into her single brother's naked, red-spotted body, she shivers in all that hotness.

Mama Sylph, Accepting

Mama Sylph didn't approve of the separation. Mama Sylph, despite her best intentions, had become accustomed to the modest riches her boys brought home every night from whatever circus or carnival came through town.

At the beginning, she was discriminating, interrogating the head carnie about the ethics and philosophies of his organization. But it didn't take long for Mama Sylph to see how very lucrative her boys were in their natural nature, in their God-given beauty. Her boys could generate a full month's income in just one night.

Of course, Mama Sylph couldn't work but a dozen hours a week, what with conjoined twins at home and something developing inside her belly, something so very demanding of both her energy and her attention, and of course, her boys couldn't go to school, not with what happened the last time people saw them.

And on top of all that, Mama Sylph wasn't a very skilled woman. Sure, she had a college degree, well, she almost had one, and for all practical purposes, she may as well have one so she told people she did because almost having one was the same as having one, she reasoned, but this almost college degree was pretty much useless in the real world. When Mama Sylph was in school, she was most interested in myths so she majored in Classics, and if she'd finished, if she didn't get pregnant with her precious boys, well, she'd be a Classicist. But now, she could hardly even remember how to count to twenty in Latin, much less Greek.

So when the Sylph family sans Papa moved from their white picket suburbia to this small town, this city right outside another city, a suburbia without the white pickets, without nosy neighbors, Mama Sylph was forced to work to pay the bills, and even though she had so few skills, and even though her boys were alone at home and even though she had a fetus named Sylvia in her belly, she worked in a Laundromat. Walking from machine to machine, she emptied quarters into a soft cloth bag. She hated it. It wasn't a difficult job, but she didn't like the whole idea of working. She found excuses not to work—the key was bent, her fingers were cramped, her head hurt, her swollen pregnant fingers couldn't fit into the slots—but soon, the city removed electricity and heat and furniture from her home, and Mama Sylph, wanting to keep up with appearances, agreed to work as her manager desired. She hated it and resented her boys for this burden and so when the head carnie came to visit her a second and third time, when he came and waved large numbered bills before her candlelit eyes—electricity seemed superfluous in comparison to other things—she didn't hesitate. Mama Sylph grabbed the bills by the fistful and shoved them away, tucking them under and behind her body, until the head carnie lacked nothing but her signature.

In a moment of compassion, Mama Sylph demanded that her boys stay with her, being so young and all, she wanted to raise them, but she promised in ink to deliver her very special boys to any event within the state or any state touching her state, so long as the carnival took care of the traveling bill.

Thus began the Sylph boys' carnival career. The boys were booked every single night of the week. They spent days and twilights driving, Mama Sylph and Sylvia singing nursery tunes, the boys crammed tight in the trunk, unable to sleep.

So yes, Mama Sylph didn't approve of her boys' separation. She made her anger apparent. She tried yelling, grounding, beating, but they were impenetrable in their single boy blisses. She tried to persuade them to reconnect, but her words echoed back and cut her cheeks with sharp lacerations. She even pleaded with Sylvia to talk some sense into her brothers, but as she spoke, Mama Sylph saw her words dissolve. Her mouth opened and closed with nothing but puffs of smoke occasionally popping out.

Mama Sylph, filled with such fierce disapproval, had no choice but to accept their separation.

Single Sylvester, Concerned

Now that Sylvester Sylph is a single boy, he is concerned. He knows it is his task to get to the center of the labyrinth, that this wasn't something Eliot just thought up, that this was something much larger than his brother or even his precious sister could have conjured. Sylvester Sylph is worried because now as a single boy, he may fail at his task. So he eagerly eats his day as a single boy, running and playing as if he were still just a boy, not someone important, not someone who could change the whole course of the world.

He will worry about that once the sun goes into hiding. He will have time worry about that later.

And the egg, aware of Sylvester's transformation, takes a nap.

Stanley is Saved

Stanley Sylph was not an only child. His papa was a busy man. He'd created another Sylph he didn't even know about. The day after Stanley Sylph committed suicide, aided by his unborn daughter Sylvia, a letter appeared in the Sylph mailbox. It had no return address and was typed on an old typewriter with a fading ribbon, such that at the beginning, the letters were light gray, but by the end, there was no color, only imprinted intentions.

The letter explained to Stanley that he had a half-sister named Susan. This half-sister of Stanley's, she was a nurse, and she wrote the letter to Stanley telling him he would be forced to commit suicide, but she would save him. Even if he never read the letter, Susan would be there just in time to bring him back to life.

The day Stanley Sylph put air into his veins, he died, but only briefly. After his wife and family drove off in their van packed with belongings and memories, a red station wagon drove up and parked. Inside this red station wagon was a beautiful woman and a little baby, all red and wrinkled, a freshly delivered baby, and the woman in the station wagon clamped her eyes hard and inside his house, Stanley Sylph coughed life back into his body. He walked outside, embraced his sister, and left that hating house in that hating town. Even though Stanley Sylph never read his sister's letter, he understood he wouldn't see his other family for a long time, that this was his new family, a family full of prophets and life.

Susan & Stanley Almost Meet

Unlike Stanley, Susan's last name is not Sylph, even though she is, technically, a Sylph. Susan's last name is Henklemeyer, a name she's not particularly proud of, but it's something she deals with. Unlike Stanley, Susan didn't grow up in a cush home, with a loving family, but like Stanley, and very much so, Susan, at a very young age, knew she was special and knew that what made her special also made her very powerful.

Susan and Stanley had very different upbringings, and even though Stanley never knew about Susan, she knew about him. She knew about the entire Sylph family. There were times she would compress minutes into days so she could watch her family, her real family, watch Stanley time himself when he got in trouble. Sometimes, Susan made herself invisible so she could walk around the Sylph home, touching this or that, smelling fresh cookies and smiles. There was something magnetic about a fresh smile to Susan, something she couldn't quite describe because in her house, her Henklemeyer house, there were no fresh smiles. On the few occasions smiles were allowed, mainly during photograph season, they came out stale and sour.

But it was not a bad childhood. Even Susan would admit this.

Mother Henklemeyer was not a mean woman, but she was intolerant, and Susan was a troublemaker. Mother Henklemeyer had eight other children that belonged to other people, eight other children other people didn't want, so by default, they belonged to her. It's true she didn't really even want them, but she was a good, Christian woman. The kind of woman who would take in a spare child she could barely afford to feed. But that child would be helpful around the house, only when needed of course.

The Henklemeyer house was always clean. It was never cluttered or dusty like the Sylph home. All eight Henklemeyer children were trained to do specific cleaning duties. Susan was taught how to wash linens, make beds (including the tightest hospital corners in the entire state), and fluff pillows. Susan is sure her decision to become a nurse was a direct result of all the beds she used to make, but despite her insistence on this autobiographical fact, in reality, she didn't make very many beds. She almost never washed linens, and she's fluffed only a handful of pillows her entire life. Although this is the truth, Susan remembers being enslaved as a child, that Mother Henklemeyer mistreated her, that her life would have been perfect had she been a Sylph, had her father, who Stanley called Papa, accepted her.

The day Stanley's papa fell off the roof and onto a wooden spike, Mother Henklemeyer was in a daze and Susan was invisible. The day Stanley's papa fell off the roof and onto a wooden spike, Stanley willed it away, the wound, the blood, the spike, and he didn't even have to close his eyes. That was the day Susan fell just a little bit in love with her half brother. Just a little bit.

Sylvia Sylph's Twin Sister

Her entire life, Sylvia Sylph has wondered where her conjoined twin was, as if perhaps she'd simply mistakenly misplaced her. Certainly, she didn't think her brothers were normal or that every person should have a conjoined twin, but there was something about them, something about their bond and physical connection that Sylvia knew she was lacking, And not only was she missing it, it was something owed to her, something she should have the chance to experience.

So Sylvia Sylph is certain that somewhere out there, she's got a twin waiting to join her, a twin who hasn't found her yet because of time or space or some other shit reason like that, but every night before Sylvia goes to bed, she closes her eyes just to see where her twin sister is and what she looks like.

Not surprisingly, it's like looking in a mirror. Surprisingly, once a year, her sister changes her appearance, changes it instantaneously and it stays that way for the whole year. Sylvia loves this about her sister, her arbitrariness: there is no pattern, no reason for the shift, it just happens, whimsically. She thinks this makes her a perfect twin sister, an ideal fit for beautiful Sylvia Sylph.

She knows they will meet one day, and from that day on, they will never be separated again. Sylvia can accept that maybe her twin sister will not like this, perhaps this will be something that takes some adjusting time, but these are minor problems, really.

Yet Another Rumor, Dispelled

It's been said that mermen have hotter blood than men, but this is not true. Even storytellers have verified this is a myth. Still, many believe.

It's easy to understand the believer's logic. Many see mermen, with their impenetrable anger and wrath, and misinterpret this as "hot-blooded." Certainly, this is a mistake. It is true they are "hot tempered" but this does not affect the physical temperature of their blood.

There are others, however, who believe the exact opposite, that merman have much colder blood than men, and they believe this for practically the exact same reason. This seems at once counterintuitive and logical. (They also have the obvious reason that mermen live under water, and it is assumed that they, like most other aquatic creatures, are cold-blooded.)

But let us dispel these myths right now. Mermen and men have the exact same blood temperature level. For all practical purposes, mermen may as well be man.

The Angry Sylph Boys

After the Sylph boys divided, they played for days until days completed their cycles so quickly the boys lived full days as if they were minutes. They played together, learning every sport and game, taking dance lessons. They played apart with women who just weeks before had touched their bodies in disgust and admiration. The Sylph boys laughed as they came, and their laughter was spiteful, as though all those years as a two-headed boy had filled them with such anger that now that they were separated, they had to enact revenge for all their suffering. Their laughter was so spiteful, the women in their beds became frightened, withdrawing naked bodies behind drapes of clothing. But this was not enough. The boys' laughter burrowed through any barricade, deafening ears with a deepness so voluptuous, so full, that dribbles of blood pooled around the women.

This went on for days and days. Perhaps even months. It's difficult to distinguish time when it moves with such rapidity, but the Sylph boys didn't let Sylvia's tricks lessen their joy. They didn't allow her to influence their desire for revenge.

The Sylph Boys Have a Heart to Heart

Just one day of physical separation, and the Sylph boys are losing their collective memory. Their singular memories—that's fine—but anything they experienced together is beginning to erase. Their earliest memory is the day they chose to be conjoined. Their father, a man they barely remembered even when they were double boys, appeared in their small, unformed ideas and persuaded them to hold each other tight. They were, at this point, not even fetuses. They had no body, and even as ideas, they were scattered, barely coherent, but they remember their father's words and when they were given bodies, they held each other with such force, with such passion, that their bodies melted together. But this memory is losing its clarity. Eliot's version has all the movement without sound, and Sylvester's version had nothing but blaring sound; no shapes or shadows accompany it.

The Sylph boys notice their tainted memories immediately. Even though they are busy experimenting with the boundaries of their new bodies, they know this is something important, something they must discuss immediately.

Eliot, swinging violently on the jungle gym, says, "It's not right."

Sylvester, letting gravity slide his body through tubes of metal, says, "It has to do with the egg. I'm sure of it."

Eliot says, "What egg?"

Sylvester says, "You know, the egg you put in the labyrinth."

"What egg?" Eliot repeats. "I didn't put anything in the middle of the maze."

Sylvester says, "It's waiting for us. For me, at least, but I think it's waiting for both of us, and I think maybe that's why we've separated."

Eliot says, "What about Sylvia? This egg sounds like something Sylvia could've made."

"I think whoever made this is bigger than Sylvia. Think about this, El. The thing we can't remember anymore has something to do with our dad."

"I hate it when you call me El."

"I'm sorry, El, but this is important."

"Stop it. Stop calling me El."

"OK, El. Whatever."

"Stop it! Stop it, or else I'm going to start calling you Slyster."

"You wouldn't!"

And the Sylph boys chase each other around the primary color painted concrete tunnels. Eliot runs into the red one to hide. Sylvester jumps over the yellow one. They continue to run and laugh and have fun. This is their day for fun, and they should not be judged for it. They run through the sand pit, over the grassy hills, and swing their bodies on the swing set, jumping at the apex and landing on their single-boy feet. They laugh, and their laugh is greater than Sylvia's. They laugh and people who hear it begin to weep. People try to take the boys' chuckles and grab them by the handful to savor their happiness, but these people, these people who try to steal the Sylph boys' happiness, they can't handle it. They don't have the strength to hold it so they weep. They weep as they watch the laughs and giggles escape, the joy they once held in their hands sliver up and away.

Not the First Love

Certainly, theirs' was not the first love, and it was definitely not the first time there was love between man and merman. But it had been a long time, so long in fact, that the very notion of interspecies love seemed impossible, and not just impossible, but abnormal, immoral, disgusting. Not that mermen were fond of morals, but they did have their standards.

It is said mermen can't feel love, that centuries before the Ed brothers were even born, mermen ordered the Evolution Council to remove their capacity for love. In fact, the only way the Ed brothers knew about love was through the far-fetched memories of poets, and storytellers quickly snatched at the opportunity to verify that yes, there was a time when mermen felt this powerful emotion called love, but now it was a complete impossibility. It was so far gone that no merman could even remember what it felt like. The closest emotion mermen felt to love was the vague sense of brotherly camaraderie for their other halves.

And yet, Edward felt this and a great deal more for Emily, this man he hardly even knew but for her faint shadow from the sky. Edward knew this was love, this stabbing sensation in the palms of his feet, this twisting of his gall bladder.

Edward felt this and a great deal more for Emily, this pathetic creature who couldn't even resist his brother's lame attempts at hypnosis. He hated the way she blindly listened to him, following his instructions like they were law, using fingers as shovels digging at her nub senses, her wings pushing against the water, unable to create movement. No, Edward shouldn't love this man, he shouldn't feel anything for her, but he couldn't help it.

Such was the love Emily would never know about, a most altruistic and kind love that would save her pathetic life.

Certainly, theirs' was not the first love, this love between Emily and Edmund, but it was a sacred love, one that would start a whole revolution, a clash of the species, all because one man fell deep into the ocean searching for the source of a voice, tender in its sadness.

Susan Makes a Tough Choice

The day Chloe was born, Susan Henklemeyer made a tough decision. She knew Chloe would be hers, her special daughter, a daughter she alone created, without man and dirty sex—not that she was opposed to sex, but to create another human through sex seemed wrong, and not just wrong, but gross. It's true that Susan Henklemeyer worked as the assistant nurse to the head nurse the night Chloe was born, but she was no nurse. She wasn't trained in nursing, but somehow, on that fated night, she became a nurse and helped the other nurses and the doctor deliver Chloe.

The name though, it had nothing to do with her. The woman giving birth to her daughter—her precious little girl she'd made in the same way mermen used to make their offspring, with her own body, giving up her own body for another—did nothing. She was, in fact, in the hospital that night for an appendectomy. She was a pretty lady who was in a lot of pain, and Susan, in her infinite kindness, opened this woman's legs and put her daughter, egg still intact, deep inside, as far as her arms could reach. This poor woman, moaning in pain, Susan gave her calmness, as her fingers wove a placenta and gently removed the shards of flaking shell. Inside, Susan could feel the softness, soft like cashmere or velvet, and she knew it was time.

Certainly, time was limited, and this poor woman's appendix was already bloated while the baby inside her, this baby she had no knowledge of, was crowning. Susan cried for help, and all too quickly, this woman was birthing her daughter, and Susan was watching, watching as the small head burst out, wrinkled and red, and right then, Susan fell in love with this wrinkled, red glob, barely formed and still somehow perfect.

But of course, Susan assisted. She helped the handsome doctor yank her darling baby out of this crying woman. She handed him the scissors to disconnect the baby from her food source, a cut so clean it was almost as if there was no connection, no bond between mother and daughter. Then, Susan thread the needle she needed to sew up the incision which had been necessary to remove her daughter, all of this, and this woman, this new mother screaming, and then, Susan remembered about the appendix.

The day Chloe was born, Susan Henklemeyer inadvertently let a woman die, but before she died of a ruptured appendix, she whispered the name Chloe. All of the nurses in the room believed it was sign, believed this woman wanted, more than anything in the world, to name her newborn daughter Chloe, and Susan, being a kind woman, granted this woman her final request. Later, when Susan walked back into the room containing both the dead Chloe and very much so alive baby Chloe, to show the other nurses how the dead woman's name was in fact Chloe, that there was no hidden message, no final desire to name her child, the other nurses were so saddened by their misinterpretation, not for the death of a woman but for misunderstanding her last word, they didn't even notice the new baby's last name.

It was a difficult choice Susan made, which patronymic to give her daughter: her own name, which she despised, or her rightful name, the name she deserved. Susan was supposed to be a Sylph, it was her right, and yet, she couldn't decide which name to write on the birth certificate. She couldn't decide which name her new daughter, Chloe, should own.

Henklemeyer

Susan Henklemeyer hated her last name. And it would've been one thing if there was some kind of lineage involved, if there had been some connection between her blood and the blood of any Henklemeyer, but as it turned out, there wasn't.

Still, this woman who gave her the most hideous name—who could possibly love the name Henklemeyer?—she would be her mother until Susan could conjure a plot to reunite with her real family.

Susan remembers thinking this.

She remembers everything that's ever happened to her, almost as if instead of organs, she had lockers to safeguard and store her history.

The Worse Changes

He has been called Edmund the Worse for as long as he can remember. It has been so long, in fact, that Edmund is certain that the Worse part is a natural part of his name.

Edmund the Worse, for as long as he remembers, has been concerned with the Worse part of his name. In truth, he was the more evil brother, but Edward was practically saccharine, and in comparison to him, any person, regardless of species or subspecies, would be considered less sweet or kind or whatever description one would like to insert. It was virtually impossible to compete for "good" traits against Edward. Such was his nature.

But one day, Edmund heard a click in his brain, something akin to a switch clipping plastic against plastic, and his typical day forever changed. Before, his days, as far back as he remembered, were spent torturing his prisoner and all other beings around him. And just like that, just a small click and he's not the Worse anymore. Edmund, in the middle of whispering evil tortures to a little man struggling with her little red wings in a cocoon of hot, stopped, and for the first time ever, he noticed something desirable in this little man, something quite attractive and perhaps even a bit lovely.

Another Caveat

We cannot be held responsible for any inaccurate translations of names. All these characters, they are archetypes to us. These humans, all of them, they are gods to us, and we must worship them, nurture them, for without us and our unflickering devotion, surely, they would disappear, like how no one remembers there was a time the ocean was not salty. We must ensure memory remains, no matter how skewed that memory is, no matter how romanticized it becomes, it must stay in our collective consciousness because as long as we remember, there is hope. It matters not how much we distort. We are nothing more than poets, storing memory until someone else can come fetch it out of us, and until that time comes, we can play with the stories as much as we want. We can make evil more malevolent and we can make even the most beautiful creatures more pristine. We can make dreadful moments more difficult to endure. This is our story to manipulate until we no longer control it. This is, in fact, our duty. Memory can only linger if it undergoes perpetual evolution. Stagnant memories are the ones most easily forgotten, the ones most cleanly erased.

We say all this to explain just once more how we cannot be held responsible for any inaccuracies. It isn't our fault. We are doing only what is expected.

Bodies & Choices

The Ed brothers had nothing to do with the petition sent to the Evolution Council. They weren't told that the other mermen wanted to divide, but if they had known, they would have gladly offered their support. There was nothing the Ed brothers despised more than each other.

On the day the Evolution Council denied the petition for division, however, the Ed brothers learned about the whole endeavor, but by then, they were practically useless. That was, until the leading coalition of mermen decided they would revolt, that mermen would fight for their right to do with their bodies as they chose. One of the leading coalition members, to stir the crowd's support, rallied, "How can this arbitrary committee, this so-called Council, tell us what we can do with our bodies? They're our bodies! It's our choice!"

And the crowd, increasingly angry, chanted, "Our bodies! Our choice!"

They pumped their fists in the air showing resistance, fists of resentment, with revenge.

The Ed brothers were there, their fingers clenched tightly. They had never felt so united. They surged with the desire to be separate. They were certain they'd been wronged. They sang, "Our bodies! Our choice! Revolt! Our bodies! Our choice! Revolt!"

But mermen have short memories, and despite their very worthy attempt at remembering the cause of this demonstration, it did not take long for small groups of mermen, here and there, to drift away, their heads unable to remember why they spoke so angrily, and only the Ed brothers remained, chanting with one united voice. They too had forgotten why their fists were pumping up to the sky.

Edward sang a song deep in sadness because he looked at his brother, his best friend, and saw no future. He looked at Edmund and felt only disgust, and this was not the way it should be with brothers. His song penetrated the ocean and drifted upward to the atmosphere where one small man was flying too close to the surface of the water, where one small man felt such compassion that she used her taloned feet to dig open her eyes.

Purpose

It is said it is impossible to get to the Golden Tree without a member of the Imperial Council guiding the way, for on his own, a tree-seeker will be lost in the labyrinth. It is said somewhere deep in the maze, there is a creature so ferocious, it will eat anything whole, even animals as large as elephants, yet despite its unnaturally large appetite and amazing capacity for food, it moves silently. It is said that up to the very moment of consumption, the victim will not even know the creature is near. In that way, we suppose the creature is kind, allowing its food to die without foresight, without certain pain. This does not mean the death is painless.

We are concerned perhaps we have confused stories about labyrinths, that perhaps there exists no beast within this particular labyrinth, but it matters not because no one can even find the entrance to the maze. We can't even prove the maze exists, much less what it obscures—the Golden Tree—much less that which protects what it obscures—the beast.

We are told, however, there will be one who will enter the maze, a chosen one who doesn't need an official opening, who can travel to the center, to the Golden Tree without fear of the beast. We are told this man will get to the center and he will touch the Golden Tree and simply by touching it, it will once again come to life. But we are told this story is a myth. We know the Golden Tree has been dead for as long as man has dominated the earth, that the Evolution Council extinguished it. Still, we are hopeful that one day, perhaps this man will come and he will touch the tree, and the tree will once again turn golden, and when this happens, we are told that order will be restored, that man will not triumph over all other species, that the earth will once again be flooded with water, clean water, and the atmosphere will correct itself. There will only be clean air and water and all the species of humankind will live again, perhaps not in harmony, but they will live, and we, we will no longer be outcasts.

The Sylph Boys Dream

After a full day of single boy playing, the Sylph boys go to sleep. Their bodies begin as uncooked noodles, stiff and starchy, but as their heads wander, they limpen, soften, become saturated with dream.

Sylvester, not surprisingly, travels into his maze. This time, he is not as enamored with the grass. His feet do not demand contact with the earth. He does not wander haphazardly, letting intuition lead. He does not insist on slowly enjoying the walk. He has a mission. He must find the egg. There is an undeniable destiny involved.

Sylvester walks quickly but attentively. He steadily approaches the egg. Although he doesn't necessarily rely on his intuition to propel him forward, he doesn't ignore it either.

While Sylvester wanders, the egg flares hotness. Still miles away, he can feel the heat crawling like a beast. Suddenly and for the first time in this labyrinth, he is frightened. His chest constricts and his heart beats without any discernible rhythm.

Eliot is just a single bed away from Sylvester. Both boys are sweating in their sleep, the heat in the room tainting the air a pale shade of red.

Eliot stands in complete darkness. He has not moved since he was transported. Where he is, it's hot. Hot and dark, and Eliot dislikes both of these. He wants to leave. He wills himself away from this place, this place that manifests everything he hates, but he can't. After trying for several minutes, his chest constricts and his heart beats without any discernible rhythm.

In this moment, this one decisive moment, Eliot understands his task. He must travel in this dark land, wherever it is. He knows this because of Sylvester's scared heart. It is not something easily explained. There is a bond between the Sylph boys that comes from years of being attached, years of being twins sharing just one body, years of being best friends. In this moment, Eliot understands he must do whatever it is his dream wants in order to save Sylvester, and even though he isn't in danger yet, he will be.

Eliot lets his heart palpitations calm, and with every beat, a small light glitters, a light just vague enough for him to see his feet. Eliot walks slowly, letting his body lead his way. He doesn't know where he's going, but he keeps on walking.

Eliot's Eyes

It doesn't take long for Eliot's eyes to adjust to the darkness. He'd stood stagnant in the hot and dark for well over an hour, but now that he is moving, now that Sylvester's stirred something inside him, he can see. Eliot sees in infrared green and shadow, but mostly, it's green because of the heat. He sees through thick walls with x-ray vision, and Eliot wonders how he's gotten these new eyes, these new powerful machines that can do anything. Jokingly, Eliot asks them for a soy vanilla latte, which he gets, the drink appearing all too quickly in his right hand. But Eliot wasn't prepared, so he drops the drink. Eliot sees the steam rise up in grey shadows, dancing a rhapsody.

Meanwhile, Eliot continues to walk without a destination. He scans ahead with his new eyes, and nothing appears abnormal. He looks and it's all the same, miles of walls barricading more walls, each one twisting smooth curves. Now that he can see, he realizes he's in a labyrinth. He considers the possibility that he and Sylvester are in the same one, but he knows what his brother's maze looks like—he did create it after all—and this isn't it.

Eliot wishes his eyes to see further, and they do. He squints just a little and sees a very bright green, a green almost yellow, almost gold. Eliot rushes, now that he can see, now that he knows what his destination is. But it isn't that easy. Every time he runs, letting his intuition lead him, he hits a wall, a dead end, a cul-de-sac. So he slows down just enough to remain calm.

The Evolutionary Revolution

The Evolutionary Revolution was not a revolution about evolution. That was a front, just like the Evolution Council's denial of the mermen's petition for division wasn't a catalyst for war. This is something history has modified, or rather, the Council modified every poet's memory to reflect what they wanted, which was a war attributed to evolution. It was something of a self-fulfilling prophecy and just a little bit self-aggrandizing. The Evolution Council wanted to be great, so great that wars were fought over its final decisions.

Yes, there was the prophecy. Before the last prophet was expunged from earth by the cruelest means possible, he declared there would a war—a revolution—based on evolution that would change the course, the landscape, of the earth forever. Certainly, men and mermen alike laughed at the prophet because the earth was solid water, or at least as solid as water could be, but the Evolution Council paid attention to him. The Council saw, or at least they'd heard stories about, the way the prophet's eyes smashed so firmly together the earth shook, if only briefly. Yes, the Evolution Council was well aware of the prophecy, which was long overdue if the prophet had been right. Prophets were notorious for their tardiness.

The day the Evolution Council received the petition by the mermen asking to be divided, they were elated. Sure, they didn't want the mass destruction of the earth, but things had become too normal, too boring, and so out of pure curiosity, they denied it. Out of desire for some drama, they declared mermen were to be two-headed beings for the rest of existence.

But this isn't what caused the Evolutionary Revolution. Yes, the mermen were upset, and yes, they wanted to revolt and did in fact do so, but mermen's memory was so weak they could hardly maintain focus long enough to remember what caused their anger. It should be noted, however, that when they did war, they did so with intense passion and vigor and caused a great deal of destruction. Their spotty memories should not dampen or lessen our impression of their warring skills.

No, there were two main causes for what is now deemed the Evolutionary Revolution, neither of which is directly related to evolution. The first cause is something small, microcosmic, if you will. The first cause was the wrath Edward the Better felt for Edmund the Worse because he (the Better) was forced to deny his love for Emily because his brother (the Worse) had imprisoned her in his dreams and would not release her. The only way for Edward to protect his love was to cast a spell on his brother making him love her, thereby insuring her safety. Certainly, Edward had the moral high ground (although it is said mermen are immoral), but watching their love blossom was too much.

The second cause of the Evolutionary Revolution was something planned far away in the center of the moon. We do not know what was planned or how it was enacted, but we do know that the Imperial Council played some card, made some kind of strategic move that caused man to revolt and begin to fiercely slaughter mermen. The men killed so many mermen, their carcasses congealed. We do not know what they did, this Imperial Council, but man had never been so vicious before, murdering indiscriminately for no apparent reason. We are only glad they did not kill all the mermen at this time. That would happen later, much later, but this war, this revolution, made mermen wary and distrustful of man, and this would be the cause of another war and another war after that, until all the mermen of the ocean would be gone, until the ocean itself would be filled with salt and an unlivable habitat for any species of human.

And so the Evolution Council declared that this war, this war that hatched so many more wars, was the war prophesied by the last prophet, this war was the Evolutionary Revolution. But it wasn't. This war the prophet spoke of, either it's never going to happen or it's still coming. Maybe even soon.

Unfairness

It was unfair, the way Emily loved Edmund with such compassion. It was unfair, first and foremost, because Emily remembered the first words Edmund muttered, that he was her captor, the one who tortured her for decades. She didn't know how long she'd been trapped, only that her bones had become elastic. She didn't know how long she was trapped that way because a blink seemed to go on for years, each word was an opera. Sometimes, she would become lost in the intricate plot of just one syllable, unable to follow the movement, the cadence of spirit. More importantly, though, this love was unfair because Emily knew Edmund was not the reason she fell, that the merman who brought her here was obscured from her. But she must be loyal to this merman who tortured her. Emily loved Edmund, fully realizing he'd been the cause of her pain, but this love was a sacrifice, a biding of time until she could find the source of song.

And of course, this love was unfair for dear Edward, who sacrificed love to save her life. He spent his days watching Emily fawn over his imbecile brother, watching from the other side of their combined body. This whole time, Edward never spoke, never sang, never even smiled. He pretended he was mute or dumb or numb, and Edmund never bothered to ask if anything was the matter. Greedy Edmund didn't care. With each day Edward didn't speak, more anger built within him, more vengeance, more of a desire to kill both his brother and their love.

And certainly, if this love was unfair for Emily and Edward, it was also unfair for Edmund the Worse. He knew his feelings for Emily were unnatural. Edmund didn't want to love Emily. He didn't want to be happy. He's a merman, and mermen don't need happiness. Furthermore, they don't want it. Edmund the Worse watches as this man offers him her love, and he takes it, not because he wants it but because he can't resist it. He can't stop. He's been rewired, changed in a most fundamental way, and he can't resist the temptation of love.

In many ways, this whole love affair is most unfair for Edmund because the others had the opportunity to change, if they really wanted to. They could alter the course of their future, but they do not. These other two, they perpetuate the charade, but Edmund, he's attempted honesty and failed. He's tried to change back to the merman he was before, but he can't. Yes, it was all unfair, but somehow, it doesn't seem right: in this story, Edmund the Worse is the victim, he is the disempowered, helpless one.

Unplanned Separation

Edward the Better, so frustrated with his unrequited love, transported himself, and by default Edmund, to the center of a congregation of mermen. This particular group of mermen happened—by mere coincidence—to be joined in anger about the Evolution Council's denial of their separation. So for the first time in nearly two decades, Edward the Better spoke. When he spoke, his words came out lavender smooth. When he spoke, Emily's bones became solid again. When he spoke, he said, "Mermen! It's time to take the future in our hands! Mermen! It's time." Edward the Better said, "My fellow merman, for too long we have been forced to live with our brothers, not as brothers but as the same person, the same merman! Mermen! It's time! We must revolt! We must take back our lives!"

Edward the Better paused. He paused, and the ocean took a deep sigh.

Without Edmund's approval, Edward spread their limbs wide.

He yelled, "Mermen! Pull! If the Evolution Council won't let us divide, let us divide ourselves! Pull! Pull! Pull!"

And before any merman knew any different, there was a reverberation of "Pull!" resounding from every edge of the earth's watery surface. Before any merman knew any different, they were attached to the Ed brothers' limbs, every merman pulling with a force he did not know he had.

Emily was the only creature in the ocean who did not pull. She watched, silently praying Edward would not be hurt though she knew better. She knew they would not survive, that all of her suffering had been for nothing.

Edward the Better did not plan this. In truth, he didn't even want to be separated from Edmund. He'd only wanted to stop the pain of witnessing their love, but intentions do not matter anymore, not for Edmund, Edward, or any other merman.

Pull

Emily wasn't necessarily right, but then again, she wasn't wrong either. She was wrong when she thought they wouldn't survive that kind of separation, the very first instance of quartering in human history. Long before the Romans thought of attaching limbs to horses and using the force of forward momentum to remove parts from the whole, Edward the Better convinced his fellow mermen to enact this torture on him and his brother. And they did. His fellow mermen pulled. The Ed brothers had four clumps of mermen heaving their body apart.

Edmund the Worse, this entire time, said nothing. Some part of him knew this was the right thing to do, not that mermen had morals.

Edward the Better, this entire time, resounded, "Pull! Pull!"

The mermen, collectively, inhaled with frowns and spit out "Pull!" with their exhales, each exhale a relief of tension, a release of all the anger they'd felt as two-headed beings for so long.

They pulled until the joints loosened.

They pulled until internal organs duplicated themselves.

They pulled until the Ed brothers sprouted new limbs.

They pulled until the Ed brothers were two mermen, two complete mermen, lacking nothing but each other.

This should have been a victory, their successful separation. Mermen as a subspecies had defied the Evolution Council. They had defied creation. They made their futures, yet something wasn't right. Even the adrenaline that moved freely through their bodies felt wrong. But right then, no one cared. Two by two, mermen demanded division, and with unprecedented strength and determination, mermen became single beings. The adrenaline made each merman stronger, unnaturally so, but they didn't care.

Emily had thought that they, the Ed brothers, would not survive their separation, which would have made her suffering in vain, but they did survive, and not only that, but now, they were single. Now, finally, scores of years after she'd fallen, she could be with Edward the Better. Emily, watching the mermen peel themselves apart, was joyous. Her fear was consumed by the adrenaline of united voices.

Cold Blood

The day mermen separated, they changed their chemical composition forever. Their blood became just a few degrees colder. It was as if something new had been added to or taken away from their old blood.

Now that they were single, they had to erect walls to clarify boundaries, to make certain all mermen knew what was whose.

Even though every merman in the ocean knew something in his blood was changed, some new chemical was either added or taken away, making it just a few degrees colder, no one cared. They were a busy species now. There was much to be done, and they could not let such small things distract them from their task, their goal.

The First Story, Part II

When Sylvia was a small girl, long before she was even a girl baby—this, in fact, occurred more than eight months before she was born, just days before her father left—she heard her very first story.

If you ask her, she will tell you she remembers the story exactly as her father told it, every word in its proper place, exactly as his grandfather told his father, exactly how his great-grandfather told his grandfather when he was still in the womb and so on and so forth. But if you ask her to relay this sacred story, passed down generations of fathers to their male bellies, just to verify there was indeed a story, and yes, it is indeed the same story, she won't tell you. If you ask her to tell this great tale, even if you ask politely, she will shake her head nimbly. She will divert her left eye down to the tip of her pointed nose while you ask again and again, each time you ask, her left eye wandering just a little deeper into the pores of her nose and when you've exhausted yourself, begging her until you no longer even care about the story anymore, she will turn around and leave.

Now it is indeed odd that Stanley Sylph had chosen to tell his female daughter the story designated for male fetuses, and it is even more disconcerting if we are to believe Stanley didn't know his wife was pregnant, but if you ask Sylvia, she will tell you she remembers the story exactly as her father said it, every word in its proper place, though she will not tell you the story.

We are tempted to not believe Sylvia Sylph. We want to say that she is an unreliable character, but she is our heroine, and we cannot doubt those to whom such power is given. We do, however, hope that in her obsession with her imaginary conjoined twin, she has confused her past with that of another, and in truth there is no story, even though that possibility frightens us even more, for if she can so easily mistake one memory for another, how can we trust her future? How can we put such stake in such an unreliable prophet?

Of course, there is one other possibility: perhaps Stanley Sylph knew all along. He knew that Sylvia existed and she would murder him. He knew Sylvia would make him put air into his veins and a woman he has never met would save him. Sometimes, we wonder if this is the story he told Sylvia, and we ask her if this is the story she means to tell. But she won't budge. We are sure that if she will tell us nothing, she certainly will never tell you either, but please, if you think you can get it out of her, by all means, go ahead and try. Just know she's tough. Underneath all that sugar, she is hard. She is, after all, a Sylph.

The Sylph Boys Sweat

The Sylph boys sleep in all that heat and sweat, and the salty moisture begins to stick to their skin. They sweat and sweat, and the sweat accumulates until it is an inch thick. An inch of something and it is no longer water. An inch on each Sylph boy, like a layer of light cotton surrounding their bodies, but they are too entrenched in dream to notice. What is certain, however, is that their temperature has begun to drop. They are no longer hot, even though Sylvester moves closer to the egg and Eliot slowly approaches a tree laced with gold. The Sylph boys are changing. It seems impossible that a metamorphosis should take place now, now when there is so much at stake, but all that heat has made them sweat and the sweat united to form this layer of cashmere around them, a placenta to keep them safe.

And now, while they are in these alternate worlds of interlacing mazes, they feel safe, as if nothing could hurt them, as if this is their duty, their destiny.

Sweat, A Clarification

But of course, the sweat is not a force field. This layer of cashmere does not protect them. It would be silly of us to even think this. No, where the Sylph boys are, nothing that can truly keep them safe.

Sylvester, Killing

Sylvester is tired. He's been walking in this maze for what feels like decades. He looks down and the grass is no longer bright. Its edges have wilted, and the air is cold. Ahead, the grass remains green, but behind him, in the places he's touched, there are deep pockets of brown. He curves his lips to blow a jet of snowflakes, thick and soggy, and they fall to his feet.

He steps forward and the grass repels from him. This isn't the way it's supposed to be. Frustrated, he stops walking. He leans his body against a thick vine awning, and as if it's the first time he's ever thought of anything, he suddenly understands.

Quickly, he straightens his tired body and turns a full 180 degrees, and the grass perks right beneath his shoes, like a sponge expanding. He exhales and everything is warmth. Even his eyelids feel nice and toasty.

Edward's Head's Imaginings

It is not as Edward had expected. From his precise memories of Emily and Edmund, Edward had built grand mansions of expectation, how he imagined love should look, what it ought feel like, the way a couple should act together. Now that the masks have been removed and the players exposed, now that Emily is with the right brother, he's disappointed.

Edward is in love with an alternate existence. Edward had succinctly imagined their love, how their first moment of union would be perfect, and yet, nothing is as it should have been.

In his head, their relationship had been elaborate, decadent, practically unbearable.

In his head, their love was simple, unquestionable, confident.

But we all know this is not Edward's head anymore.

Their love is not bad. But it is a disappointment.

The Evolved Evolution Council

It is not because we want to regress that we explore the past. That would be a complete mischaracterization of our intentions. Nor are we the type to look back upon yesterday with a milky, romanticized eye, an eye that does not scrutinize, an uncritical eye.

Rather, we look to the past because we must find the errors of our ancestors. We must acknowledge their foolishness and never repeat it, but even in thinking this, we are afraid we have put ourselves on a pedestal, even as we point our pointed index fingers at them, that Council of the past. We hold our knowledge and our technology, and we scoff at them. We take our egos and say it will be our generation who we will see the war the prophet foretold, this great Evolutionary Revolution will come now, now that we are here to see it. Back then, their egos blinded them so they could hardly distinguish a small battle from a revolution.

No, that Evolution Council from eons ago, they were flawed. They were greedy. They hoarded power, and it was only fitting for the Imperial Council to form right there, right in front of them, and they had no idea. They were so invested in their own petty dramas. They didn't see the Imperial Council. In their foolish desire for war, they gave man too much power and took none of it away, never putting limitations on what they could do. That was their mistake, the mistake that practically wiped out every other species of human but man. Such is the situation now. Man dominates the earth, just as the Imperial Council planned, but the other species, they are seething right beneath the skins of man. They are waiting for the call. They are everywhere, hiding here and there, and it is only a matter of time.

No, we are not so foolish, so blind-sighted as our predecessors. We explore the past because we don't want another botched war. We must ensure that this war, this impending revolution, this is the one that will restore the earth to what it was, that it will bring humans as a species back into equilibrium and save our earth that is dying too quickly.

Today, we hoard all those other species, we listen to storytellers tell their stories, we hide poets, and protect the egg, because we know that soon, so very soon, prophets too shall rise from their hiding places among man, and when they do, we shall see the war that the very last prophet foretold a long, long time ago.

The Interconnected Sisters Meet

Sylvia Sylph ought to be concerned about her brothers, but she is too preoccupied with haunting the sister she does not have. When Sylvia concentrates for long enough and uses all her strength, she can see her sister. When Sylvia does this, she sees her sister, beautiful and naked. Sylvia doesn't want pornography, but her sister just won't wear clothes. Sylvia watches as her sister climbs on objects higher and higher in her cramped apartment, and when she reaches the top of whatever she's climbed, she falls freely. Sylvia squints her already closed eyes, anticipating the crash, but it does not come. She opens her eyes and sees her sister hovering centimeters from the floor, her little red wings flapping with the rapidity of a hummingbird.

Sylvia is enamored with her sister, the way she lets her body hover that way for minutes until her wings get tired. Sylvia watches as Chloe lies there, resting, only to do it all over again.

Then, Sylvia remembers her brothers. She apologizes to her sister, and in this moment of interconnection, she learns that her sister has a name, a beautiful name, Chloe, and her sister learns that the woman on the other side watching her also has a name, Sylvia, Sylvia Sylph, beautiful Sylvia Sylph.

Chloe Closes her Eyes

As far back as Chloe Henklemeyer can remember, every year on her birthday, her and her mother tell a story, and for that whole next year, the story becomes truth. Her mother doesn't open her eyes while they tell the story; her eyes are smashed shut and she is concentrating. As a teenager, Chloe didn't exactly know what her mother was concentrating on, but whatever it was, she was sure there was some kind of connection between this movement into deep thought and the physical change that occurred in her body for the next year.

Of course, it wasn't like Chloe had never noticed Susan smash her eyes shut before. No, this was something she'd noticed since she was a very small girl. She wanted—more than anything—to be able to change things the way her Susan did, but no matter how hard she tried, she couldn't. She did, however, possess different abilities she'd never really told anyone about, things she'd even kept hidden from her Susan. First, her eyes itched all the time, but this is something she did tell her mother, and Susan, as quick as anything, closed her eyes tight and the irritation disappeared. Next, she could look at anyone and discern anything she wanted about their past. This was something she did with StanStan all the time. She'd just look at him and immediately flash to the place StanStan lived with a different family with boys with one body but with two heads and a pretty little girl, a girl who looked just like she did, and a nice woman. Chloe could tell this because she glowed the color of kindness, but she had an exterior darkness, one of misunderstanding and greed. No one else in the family had that. This glowing woman must've been the mother, and she was a normal woman. She was nothing special, though she had to deal with a whole family of prophets and mermen. Of course, Chloe didn't know these terms. Chloe used words like two-headed boy and mind-readers, words like manipulators and writers.

And then there's the girl who looks just like Chloe, a perfect replica. Often, Chloe travels into the girl's dreams and wanders. Sometimes, she thinks maybe they can meet, but she does nothing about it.

But things are slowly changing for Chloe. She has never been able to make things different just by closing her eyes, but now that she is no longer talking to her Susan, she can. Just by smashing her eyes, she could make her wings grow. Just by concentrating the way her Susan concentrated, she finally got the nerve to tell Sylvia, StanStan's precious Sylvia, her name.

Selfishness

This is not to say Chloe is unaware of Sylvia's role in bringing StanStan to her. It is just that the entire Henklemeyer family is happy because now, there is a father figure for them to rely on. So they forgive Sylvia for her wrong-doing, but they do more than that. They thank her for her jealousy, her insecurity. They, as a family of three, a family of three Henklemeyers, are selfishly joyous.

Stanley Gets a New Name

The day Susan Henklemeyer saved Stanley Sylph, he decided he was forever indebted to her, but since he had nothing to give her, he offered to take her name, not necessarily as husband but as family. He saw, in Susan's arms, a small baby, still wrinkled red, and decided he loved her. He loved her more than he'd ever loved anything before in his entire life, except perhaps the daughter who killed him. He couldn't love anything more than her, but then again, we don't even know if he knew she existed.

What is certain, however, is that he will know and very soon. All too soon, all the masks will be dropped and the players will come to the forefront, each one bearing herself proud. But we are not there yet. This is not the day. Today is not even today yet, and this is the story of Susan and Stanley Henklemeyer, proud parents of Chloe Henklemeyer.

And today, Susan politely declines, saying she's not really one to want a nuclear family, coming from a foster family and all, but even more, she just doesn't want a man around. She says all this, and she says it with her eyes shut, but this is a trick Stanley Sylph knows too well. Before she can enter his mind to persuade him, before the edges of her eyes have the chance to crinkle intensity, his weight propels him onto his knees, and he begs. Stanley Sylph tells her it is only because of her that he is alive, and it is his duty to serve her. His father taught him nobility and servility and his father would be ashamed if he saw this situation. Stanley told her that this was the way it was supposed to be. Before the last prophet died, he'd told a story, a story he told his unborn daughter, the very same story Susan told Chloe before she was born, and this was the way it needed to be, no matter how much she resisted, it would happen just this way because it had been foretold, and there was nothing either of them could do about it.

Susan Henklemeyer, never the sentimental one, cried a little as he spoke, but then, just as quickly, she snapped. She said, "You're hardly the last prophet, and you of all people should know it. That you worship such bullshit makes me love you less, brother, but it doesn't mean I don't love you, brother. Brother Stanley Henklemeyer, you of all people should know that we never have to accept anything. We control our fates as easily as we blink."

Stanley Henklemeyer had never in his entire life felt intimidated, but just then, he was glad he was already on his knees because if he wasn't, he was quite sure he would have fallen from the impact of her words.

Stanley, Remembering

Stanley Henklemeyer loves his new life, although it's not as if he doesn't miss his previous life too. He liked Betty well enough, maybe he even loved her a little, though she hardly understood the gravity of his existence, of their boys' existence, and of course, his boys were simply spectacular. Stanley Henklemeyer loved his old life, back when he was Stanley Sylph. He alone created those boys, those magnificently connected boys who would change history. Stanley Henklemeyer didn't know how this would happen, only that it would, and his poor, stupid wife, dear, kind, easily manipulated Betty, all she wanted was to put the boys on display for the world to point their fingers at in judgment. Stanley laughs at the idea now, people pointing at his boys laughing. Stanley knows that soon, it will be his boys laughing. Soon, but not yet.

Even back when he was Stanley Sylph, he knew he shouldn't blame Betty, but when no one else was looking, he did, and when he did, he hated her fiercely. During these times, and they were quite often, Stanley would imagine Betty as a car or a microwave. As she went about her day, at his will, she would randomly honk or buzz, her hands moving involuntary like windshield wipers. Luckily, dear Betty never realized this, and luckily, these bouts didn't last long because Stanley, off in the corner laughing so hard his cheeks would scarlet, would forget and release her from his hold.

But we wouldn't want you to think Stanley was not the good or caring husband he was. He tried to be patient with Betty, but often, she just wouldn't get it. It was only during these times of ultimate frustration that Stanley manipulated her. He was hardly a cruel man, and especially not to his own wife.

And now, he's a Henklemeyer. His new life's different and he loves it. With them, he can hold nothing back, even if he'd wanted to. This pair of mother-daughter prophets, they're beautiful and they're his.

Before he'd met Susan Henklemeyer, he'd considered the possibility of others out there like him, but he'd secretly hoped there weren't. He'd wanted to be original, the one and only version of himself, and this is what he'd hoped for most often, that he was the very last in a breed, the very last of a whole subspecies of human to survive, that it was his duty, his task, to salvage more than just a lineage and a name.

Senses

The Evolution Council was unhappy when man started using her eyes again. They had done a great deal for man when she decided to seal her eyes so long ago. They had, in fact, convened a special meeting just to help man cope with the loss of one of her most valuable senses. So when man decided, just like that, to open her eyes without even conferring with the Council, well, that hurt their feelings, but they were understanding, and to prove this, they relieved man's allergy to hydrogen, and man up in the atmosphere saw clear through the oceans, straight to the other side of the earth.

The Evolution Council would later regret so much about their preferential treatment toward man. They'd regret having to take the drastic action of removing man's three additional senses without warning, without giving them advanced notice. This is the one thing they would regret most, the pivotal act that stripped their godlike power and authority. Even though this would come later, it can all be traced back to the day man started abusing her powers, the day they tacitly forced the Evolution Council to take action.

So man was shocked when she no longer felt kindness, when she suddenly learned the joy of mermen's revenge.

A Clarification of Names

Of course, back then, man was not called man. That happened later, a century or so after they'd already wiped out all other subspecies of human. Smartly, man had waited the due grieving period—until every last man on earth did not know that other subspecies had ever existed, which meant all memory of the past was slated clean—before he truncated human into man. It was not altogether original, but man was never known for her originality.

Back before all of this horror and terror, back before they were called man, they were known as martyrs. Now, certainly, that word is emblazoned with strings and caveats, as if humankind does not want to forget what kindness can do, but so much memory has been altered we are left with simple words and characteristics, none of which have much meaning.

And yes, mermen were not always called mermen. This is a modern term used so people can understand notions of people living beneath the surface of water. Mermen, actually, were the subspecies known as man because they were the most populous subspecies; however, they were also called saints, a term all too prophetic. These words carried none of the same connotations as they do today. Back then, they were the original, and today, today we've usurped these words and bastardized their intention as much as we can.

The Evolution Council Evolves Man

Unlike mermen, who were hermaphroditic because they possessed too much sex, men were eunuchs. Out of pure pity, the Evolution Council deemed man would be gendered female, so they would not feel too left out during the wars and battles between the sexes. Perhaps this is why the Council loved man so much, because she was constantly a misfit of a subspecies, the one that survived outside of water, the one cast off to the corner to play all by herself.

Looking back, this was certainly a misinformed sympathy, but the Evolution Council were not gods. They did not possess omniscience. They were flawed humans, as we all are, and even if they did possess the power of gods, they did not have the authority or knowledge that should come along with it. We cannot judge them for their lack of foresight.

But man was not woman. She did not possess modern conceptions of physical femaleness or other notions of femininity. She did not have an hourglass figure, breasts which spout milk for food, or hair. Man, back then, was all skin. The temperature, being so temperate, did not require hair to trap warmth. Back then, man looked like a block with little red wings attached to either her hips or her thighs. She was raw and ugly, but man did not care about appearances. She had no one to impress.

During that very same session, the mermen's petition to divide their bodies was denied. It is said that the mermen's suggestion catalyzed a discussion about man's body among the Council. As the story goes, the Council declared with their very definitive stamp that mermen could not separate, that they were doomed to a life of two-headedness, and with that same apocryphal stamp, the Evolution Council gave man something she had never asked for: sex, and two of them at that.

Man Full of Senses

Once they were given sex, half of the population became greedy, half the population was constantly hungry for more, and according to many storytellers, it was this greed that made them use their taloned feet to remove the cemented mucous sealing their eyes. Hence, there was man, endowed with eight senses and sex, and it is only fitting that they became cocky, that suddenly, they had notions of divinity and immortality.

It was only a matter of days before there was war.

Looking back, we want to attribute these first few battles, these insatiable desires, to man's concern for Emily, but too much time had lapsed and Emily had become a forgotten treasure caught in the middle of ocean. We want to think that man still wanted to save Emily, but this wasn't the case. When they gained sex, they tasted power, and no matter what the Evolution Council would do, things would never be the same. Even after the Council took away those three extra senses, the world was already doomed to a future dominated by this new form of man, this new, powerful beast.

And Emily, still caught under the water, she wasn't even an afterthought. It was almost as if they had no recollection of her existence, as if she was nothing more than a dream.

Confusion

We are trying to keep things in order, but it is becoming increasingly difficult to keep tabs on one poet's memories because they conflict with another poet's memories, which agree with this one poet's but not that other poet's version of the past. There are so many poets with so many memories, and then, there are the storytellers. We are trying our hardest to keep things straight, but we are becoming confused and frustrated with all these tales, and we are trying to decipher the most truthful history, but with so many variations, time itself becomes arbitrary, and even the players have lost a certain distinction, their unique characteristics completely lost for the sake of a temporal accuracy which we cannot ensure. This does not mean we do not try because we do, but trying alone will not get us any closer to the Golden Tree and trying will not make our precious egg hatch. Our attempts are only meant to clarify, but in this clarification, we grow more confused.

A Loss of Wings

It was a gradual shift. Emily, being under water for so long, eventually lost her wings.

But it was nothing like modern stories of angels losing their wings, a vengeful but understanding god painstakingly taking them away because of the angel's irreparable, unforgivable crime, a crime that this vengeful but understanding god has tried, lord knows he's tried, to forgive, but it's impossible.

What Emily experienced was not damnation or punishment.

Nor was it something the Evolution Council declared.

Rather, Emily's loss of wings, this gradual degradation, was the first instance of true evolution to occur since the formation of the Evolution Council. She experienced evolution the way it was intended, naturally.

The truth is the Evolution Council changed species for the sake of change. Most often, alterations were completely arbitrary, something some species dreamed during a midday nap, and the Council would look over the petition, counting signatures and checking for grammatical errors, and just as arbitrarily, it was either approved or denied.

We want to think there was some grander purpose for this or that evolutionary change, some semblance of a bigger scheme, but no, back then, the Evolution Council considered themselves gods, and they applied their power liberally amongst their many minion.

And the slow disintegration of Emily's wings, this was something altogether unapproved.

Emily Becoming a Merman

Emily, without wings, was no different from a merman. Sure, there were certain fundamental anatomical disparities, but for all practical purposes, she had been under the surface of the ocean for so long that any manlike characteristics (or martyr, if you will) had cleanly dissolved into the water.

There are many who say it was the dissolution of her martyr senses into the water that made the ocean salty. This is a thrilling option, if only it were true.

Emily's gradual shift in physical, mental, and psychic body was certainly detrimental to the ocean and the world at large, but it was nothing so great as to change the chemical composition of the ocean.

We wish it were that simple—we really do—but we cannot support rumors ungrounded in truth.

What is most important, however, is how Emily was slowly becoming a merman. It wasn't just her wings falling off or shriveling away, whatever way you want to imagine them leaving, her mind was changing too, her senses reformed to deformity, as if she actively chose to go against the methods of the Evolution Council.

Man, Advancing

A century or so after man wiped out all other varieties of human, they began building. They took inventory of what had been lost and what could be replaced. Unfortunately, every man who had lived when other kinds of human still existed had long since died, and their memory was recorded on paper, in narrative form, a much less accurate method than poets. These narratives were often exaggerated tales of two-headed beasts hundreds of feet tall and angelic men with wings of the most pure white, full of soft feathers and flowing blonde locks. These narratives recounted how these beasts virtually pulled themselves apart with brute strength, and man could simply not compete against them physically and had to resort to cunning, a skill which she developed because she was the preferred species. These narratives tell of shape-shifters, avatars, sinking into borrowed skin and cannibalistically eating their new bodies until no semblance of its previous owners remained. These were narratives of war and pain filled with men falling from the sky like rain, the decomposition of bodies in the ocean, a pure and clean ocean—stories of suffering and captivity, terrorism and victory.

But they never tell of the time right after the war ended. That is not a pleasant story. There is no hero, no savior. In the days after the war ended, there was only destitution, carcasses piled into mounds so hot and so large they sunk to the middle of the earth and molded into rot. No one tells this story. This is not something anyone wants to remember, yet somehow, we have its remainders, a skeleton refusing erasure.

We do not know exactly what happened, but we have nonetheless arranged a rough timeline accounting for the possibilities, and certainly, while we do not claim to have it all correct, it is a beginning. It is what we have, until poets produce a singular story without inaccuracies, until storytellers offer a response we understand, a response we like.

The pile of rotting bodies exuded a pungent fume, and the sun was particularly harsh, shining straight through the water onto the dead bodies, cooking them, and it is said that the bodies sizzled, even in the water, as the surviving men swam laps around the pile, trying to cool it off, trying to undo the damage of the sun. But the swimming only created more movement, and soon, the bodies were a rotating mass. The heat was unbearable. The stench even worse. Man had to swim further and further away just to avoid the smell.

But the farther man moved from the mass, the larger it grew, until man had to take shifts to make it all the way around. To assure there was no cheating, man passed either a tibia or fibula to account for the number of swimmers at any time, but man, being crafty, found caveats in the rules, and soon, there were just a few men swimming, a few men carrying scores of bones, their movement slow only because of the weight tied to them, and the mass, the center of the earth started extending. It was not long before man could not make full laps around this mass anymore. It was not long until man began to crawl on this hard mass, this accumulation of death.

By the time man started crawling, there was no longer any memory of war, no memory of the mass genocide, no memory of a time when man, full of kindness, flew eyeless in the atmosphere. But even though they couldn't remember, man knew there were certain pieces missing. For instance, they had no way of recording legacy. Hence, writing was created, and it began from the most unpretentious seed, a simple stick on the ground soft from the saturation of blood. When all the soil of the earth was permeated with writing, they were forced to other means, all the while, still concerned with the accuracy of these stories. But there was nothing they could do about it then. This is an invention we still struggle with today.

Man developed many new things for the sake of legacy. They planted trees so they could cut them down and make paper. They made mountains to hide precious metals. They made ships and cars, computers and iPods, hats and clothes. Still, with all of these technological developments, they could not verify truth, they could not discern fact from lie, and because of this, they have no recollection of their past. They have no clue about prophets and messages of revolution because long ago, they wiped storytellers into hiding.

So man with his progress, his greatness, exposes his most detrimental flaw.

The Egg's Parents

It is true that we love the Ed brothers and Emily, but our fondness for them cannot change history. We have devoted so much of our lives to uncovering their lives, their legacies. We have grown old with them, fallen in love with them, and now, out of love, it is time to accept their deaths, for we will not die with them, not when we have their egg.

This is not something we say lightly. We have, since the very first appearance of the egg, hoped and secretly prayed that it is somehow a part of them, our Edmund, Edward, and Emily, perhaps their progeny, perhaps even an incarnation of them and their story. We have wanted this, though we knew it was a petty desire. We knew these three were killed, massacred, with all the other mermen. The day man dove into the ocean, they began killing indiscriminately. We know Emily pleaded, explaining how she was one of them, but by this time, the Evolution Council had stripped man of his other senses. They heard the desperation in her voice, her burrowing cries, but they ignored it. They were immune to it.

We know that Emily was killed just like any other ordinary merman, and that both Edmund and Edward died before her, trying to protect her.

All of this was verified by any number of poets and storytellers.

But one appeared only yesterday saying he was the last poet, the very last one, the only one who witnessed the massacre in its entirety. He said before the Ed brothers and Emily died, they had created an egg, and it was not a solitary act. Anticipating the impending war, they birthed an egg with parts from all three of their bodies, and they spun it with such force that it was catapulted out of the ocean. It broke the atmosphere with its hard shell. This poet said the three of them promised that mermen would have their revenge, and this egg, their child, would reappear, and when it hatches, it will release centuries of pent up revenge on all men and their progeny.

We do not like this possibility, yet we cannot wait for it to happen. We are not scared. We are not man. We are exempt from the merman's wrath.

So we covet their egg and wait.

The So-Called Evolutionary Revolution

First, what has been called the Evolutionary Revolution was not the Evolutionary Revolution.

Second, man, endowed with sex and his eight senses, dove into the ocean, wanting more than just the skies and the moon, and the mermen did not like this possibility of sharing. They felt this was a personal attack, and feeding from an anger already present from the Evolution Council's preference to man, they began killing.

Then, man retreated. The Evolution Council, finally accepting their errors, took away man's extra senses and restored his allergy to hydrogen.

Man, with an intense burning in his eyes, dove back into the water. He killed without care, as if kindness was something he had never experienced. Mermen fought with tenacity, but man, suddenly unburdened by care or kindness, unleashed a wrath unparalleled to any the earth had seen before or has seen since.

Yes, mermen were not the most ideal subspecies, but even they did not deserve man's rage.

From the history presented, there is no way this war could have been called a revolution and it had nothing to do with evolution, except that every bit of it had some tie to the Evolution Council and their decisions. But this was no Evolutionary Revolution. It was a mass extermination, and it was disgusting.

Chloe Defines Prophet

Chloe is sure her mother is a prophet, but not the type of prophet most people think of when they use that word. People mostly speak of prophets as fortune-tellers, forecasters of fate, and usually, in a religious sense. This is not what Chloe means. She does not think her mother translates the future. Her mother makes the future.

To Chloe, the word prophet has a historicity to it, and even though she doesn't necessarily know its full story, she can easily tap into its past. It's a skill she has. Chloe can see parts of anybody's past, keystone moments, mundane daily tasks, the pieces that create personality, but she can only do this to people.

That is, until the word prophet.

It seemed innocuous at first. She was looking through a dictionary for some word or another, and when her little fingers scanning the page paused briefly over the word prophet, she saw scenes of war and trial. She felt the pain of burning flesh, not from fire but from internal heat, a hotness radiating from marrow, and bone itself, she felt it split into tiny fractures. Chloe Henklemeyer saw a world brimming with diaphanous water as far as her eyes could reach, and she saw kindness in variant shades. Chloe took all this in. Then, she opened her eyes and continued moving her fingers as though nothing had happened.

The next time her fingers wandered by the word, she caught glimpses of her Susan and StanStan. She saw them and felt the pain of extinction.

So she said the word prophet out loud. As she spoke, she saw the life of a girl who looked just like her, but wasn't. It was some other girl, a girl who could be her twin sister. This was the first time Chloe met Sylvia Sylph, a girl she imagined as an imaginary friend, but from that day on, prophet became her favorite word, one that united her to her family and a new friend, one who held so many possibilities.

Mama Sylph Goes to Bed

Mama Sylph enjoys sleeping. It's late in the Sylph home, and it's hot. It's so hot, in fact, that Mama Sylph considers turning on the air conditioner. Instead, she takes off all her clothes and stretches her naked body out on her king sized bed. She roles around, moaning as the tip of a pillowcase hits her clitoris just right. It's a nice feeling, this accidental masturbation, but she must control it, control herself, or she'll likely be screaming orgasms in a matter of seconds. It's been a long time, and Mama Sylph wants to control herself, but she doesn't. She realizes she has no reason to hold back. So she allows herself this one small pleasure, this one small moment of relief, a time finally for herself.

Besides, her boys have been asleep for God knows how long, and the truth of the matter is there's a part of Mama Sylph that hates her boys. It's odd. She knows it makes her a hypocrite, hating them so much, but she can't deny the way she feels. The truth of the matter is she wants her boys to be separate, to be single boys. For most of their lives, she never wanted to be the mother of freaks. She didn't want to move here or move there because some ignorant assholes saw her boys and laughed. But most of all, she knows Stanley committed suicide because of them. And it's her fault the boys turned out that way, deformed and ugly, making her husband, her only support, kill himself. It was their fault for being connected, for coming out of her that way, that unnatural way.

Yet she has to admit, she's gotten used to the money, that without their, let's say, unique disposition, she would have to work a regular job. And she's used to it, the way they look, their unattractiveness. She's used to patting them on their freak heads and saying they're beautiful without meaning it. She's used to lying, and now what? Now they're no longer connected, and they're attractive. They are beautiful boys. In some ways, Mama Sylph thinks it's wrong, how pretty she thinks her boys are, but they are so pretty. It's true. They are. They're gorgeous. Most nights, now that the boys are two boys instead of one, Mama Sylph has special dreams about them. It's not something she'd want to admit. In fact, it's something she struggles with every night, the desire to sleep so she can get even closer to her boys. It's disgusting. She knows it's repugnant, definitely wrong, but Mama Sylph has been a widow for a long time, and pleasure only comes when her conscious mind is turned off, when she cannot control herself.

Sometimes, she wishes she could be like Stanley.

Yes, of course she knows about Stanley's magic powers. A wife knows things, even if he did his best to hide it from her. Sometimes, she even blames him for being dead because if he'd really wanted to, she's sure he could have come back to life. He just had to want it enough. Instead, he'd let himself die, just like that, and now, she's got these two unconnected boys who she dreams about and Sylvia, her precious Sylvia, just like her papa.

Sometimes, she wants to ask Sylvia to make them rich. She knows Sylvia could do it, if she wanted to, but she doesn't want to exploit her darling daughter that way.

It's just that she's so tired, thinking about dreams and sleep and her unconnected boys and her daughter who can stop time. She's caught in this cycle of this and that, and there's not much she can do about it, so she decides to sleep. Yes, she should sleep now.

Except now, she's cold.

Sylvia, Feeling Left Out

Sylvia Sylph thinks this moment in time is a nexus, a time of intersections absolutely integral to the future of the earth. This moment requires perfect choreography. She doesn't want to be melodramatic, but it's the truth.

Sylvia is quite possibly the most knowledgeable character. She may know more than we do, which isn't necessarily problematic, but it does hinder us a little. But let us explore some of the things Sylvia knows. For instance, Sylvia knows Sylvester is going toward an egg that holds much more than its exterior shows. She does not, however, know what is inside the egg. She knows Eliot is traveling toward the Golden Tree, but she does not know the significance of the tree. She does not know its history. She also knows her father and his sister and their daughter are traveling towards us. This is something we do not know yet, or at least, we didn't know until right then. Sylvia chooses to reveal small details to us as she wishes. She knows we are at her mercy for snippets of information, things we couldn't possibly learn ourselves, things she changes on a whim because she can, because sometimes, she likes to throw us off with a simple snap.

But enough about us. This is about Sylvia, and right now, she wants her brothers to be safe, but she can't control their fate. It's too late. If she'd wanted to protect them, she should have never let them split. She knew it would happen, and she could've stopped it and kept them safe by keeping them together, but she didn't. And right now, because she can't control her brothers, she wants to see her sister instead. But her sister is on a journey with her family, which is really

Sylvia's family too. Right now, she wishes her mama wasn't so pathetic, but we think she secretly basks in it. It's no surprise Sylvia resents her mama and for no particular reason. Right now, Sylvia wishes she were more important, that she could really affect something, and she doesn't realize she already has, probably more so than anyone else, but this isn't enough for her. She wants the spotlight constantly, and sometimes, there just isn't enough light to go around. Perhaps this is why Eliot is caught in a maze of perpetual darkness, why Sylvia had to make herself useful by giving him both night and x-ray vision. She's happy to play a part in this unraveling. It makes her feel special.

A Reunion

The mother called the daughter. When she didn't pick up the phone, the mother became worried and quickly rushed over to her apartment. The daughter was just in the shower and didn't hear her phone ring. Still partially wet but so happy to see her mother, as it has been months since the two have seen each other, a side-effect of a botched birthday year, the daughter exclaimed, "My Susan! It's so wonderful to see you!"

The mother noted the little red wings very calmly resting at the daughter's side. Then, she reached out her left hand and touched one. They weren't frightened. They were confident. They nudged toward the stroke. The mother smiled at this. She knew this meant her daughter was strong. Her daughter was ready.

The mother said, "My darling it has been so long, and to celebrate our reunion, we're going on a trip."

The daughter, not at all surprised, said, "When?"

The mother said, "Now."

The daughter said, "Where?"

The mother said, "To find the Evolution Council."

The daughter did not seem bothered by this at all. She said, "Is StanStan coming?"

The mother said, "He's driving."

The daughter said, "But will this stop me from falling in love?"

The mother said, "This is the only way you can fall in love."

The daughter said, "Do we have time for me dry off?"

The Agricultural Moon

A long time ago, before the earth was filled with land and before the ocean was salty, man flew in the air and mermen swam in the clean ocean, vengeful as ever. During this time, because the whole earth was nothing but water and atmosphere, man flew to the moon, which was not the dead satellite it is today. Back then, the moon was arable, and on the moon, man grew two kinds of fruit and three kinds of vegetables, and she survived joyously with this variety of food for most of her existence.

Then, the Evolution Council gave man sex.

Then, man grew a diverse forest of fruits and vegetables, and the earth, being a translucent ball save for the shadow of mermen, filtered just the right amount of sunlight, making the moon a most ideal spot for farming.

Man created variations of flora, splicing this bud with that leaf, and soon, the moon was covered with more variety than man could conceivably even sample, but man was diligent with their required three hours of daily moon labor and continued their genetic splicing until no recognizable species of food still existed from their collective childhoods. In the matter of just one generation, their hybrid, bio-engineered foods controlled the entire moon.

Of course, it was not long after this that the so-called Evolutionary Revolution occurred and the moon and all her floral splendor was rendered useless.

Imprisonment

The mother knocked on her daughter's door, and when she did not answer, the mother broke the most sacred of rules: she entered the room without permission. But that's not all. No, this was a snoopy mother, one who wanted to uncover secrets rolled up and jammed in the back of drawers, under beds, or iron-flattened and hidden between mattresses. This mother wanted to know all her daughter's secrets, which was why the daughter had created the pact, the mother-daughter pact, that the mother shall not enter the daughter's room and snoop, lest she suffer consequences equal to the weight of the crime. Normally, mothers would not stand for such rules, but this was no ordinary daughter. This was no ordinary family. This is the Sylph family, a family full of prophets and mermen, save the mother, who was nothing more than an ordinary human being.

When the mother knocked on her daughter's door, she didn't know Sylvia was busy watching over her brothers.

Early in the morning, after a healthy night's sleep, the mother knocked on her daughter's door to ask if she wanted pancakes or eggs for breakfast, and when the daughter didn't reply, the mother, eager in her quest for knowledge, hastily opened the door, and the room was empty. It was almost as if there wasn't a daughter, as if every part of Sylvia Sylph had disappeared. The mother opened the closet door. Nothing. There was nothing in the entire room. The mother let go of the doorknob to the closet, and the whole closet evaporated. The room was nothing but walls and a floor and one door leading out of the room. The mother became frightened and ran toward the exit, but her feet weren't as quick as Sylvia's mind and the door vanished. Then, the mother understood. Her daughter was not one to be reckoned with.

It is unclear how long the mother stayed in the daughter's room, banging on the walls with a might even she did not know she had. The mother kicked the walls, thinking she could at least break through the cheap drywall, but the daughter had replaced it with concrete, and the mother broke at least a few of her toes.

So the mother stayed in her daughter's empty room, and she slept and woke and slept and woke in more cycles than she could count. The mother tore off her clothes in strips until she wore nothing but undergarments. Then, she tore those off in inch-sized squares. The mother eventually stopped bothering to move around. She lived in one position, her legs open, her knees bent in angles, her torso upright. Had she not looked so pathetic, she could have assumed the shape of a dancer, limbering her body before a ballet, but the mother was no dancer. She sat in the center of a circle of shit, which after she defecated, she would push away from her body, but only as far as her arms could reach. She let her urine remain as it was. Considering the amount of piss and shit around her, she was never hungry. This was nothing that concerned her. She knew she would not die here. This was a punishment, and as soon as Sylvia decided she had paid her penance, a door would appear and all of this would dissolve into Sylvia's perfectly clean room, a room which held secrets the mother would never know.

Layer by Layer

Sylvia Sylph kneels between her brothers, a hand on each one. Her fingers dig in a cyclical motion until a small whirlwind appears around each of her digits. Sylvia doesn't like this, how her brothers have this layer of soft cotton around their bodies, and she struggles to remove it. She isn't sure why, but she intuits whatever this is, it's not good. Even though it looks like a cocoon, it isn't keeping them safe. This thing will make them emerge as something entirely different, something entirely not themselves. Sylvia Sylph digs. When she finally gets a good grasp on a large chunk fiber, she pulls gently to unravel it. She de-mummifies them, layer by layer.

As she gets closer to the bodies beneath, as their shapes become apparent, she can see that down there, down beneath all that cashmere, they have already changed. It is nothing obvious. Externally, they look more or less the same, close enough that their mama wouldn't be able to tell the difference, but Sylvia knows it immediately. Externally, other than the excess covering, they are still Sylvester and Eliot, but Sylvia knows better than to trust externalities. She understands this journey has changed something inside, that they are chemically different, as if someone had just dumped a bucket of salt into their blood, altering their composition forever.

Still, Sylvia is not scared for them. She is confident this change is needed, that they are fulfilling their task, and although she has no idea what this task is, she's sure this shift in body is necessary if they are to survive, and she loves her brothers desperately enough to want them to live.

Satisfied, Sylvia opens her eyes to free her mama, and still with one hand on each brother, she wills them more strength because she knows they will soon meet beasts no man has seen before, beasts that have no name and very few weaknesses.

A Moment between Two Brothers

Sylvester and Eliot Sylph, each in their respective maze, feel a sudden surge of energy and power. They both feel smarter and faster, and strangely enough, more connected, more in tune with each other. Running Eliot can feel Sylvester touching a wall, the texture of wet cement on his fingertips. Sylvester touching the wall feels movement in his motionless, tired feet.

The brother screams, "Eliot! Can you hear me?"

The brother says, "Not so loud, dude. I'm right here. I can hear you."

The brother says, "It's coming, isn't it?"

The brother says, "Yeah, I think so. Hey Ester, I'm scared."

The brother says, "It'll be OK. And stop calling me Ester. You know I hate that."

The brother says, "Whatever man. Why'd you even call me?"

The brother says, "Do you believe in beasts? Do you think they'll come after us? Do you think Sylvia's right?"

The brother says, "She's never been wrong before."

The brother says, "I'm scared."

The brother says, "We have to keep going. That's why we're here. We don't a choice."

The brother says, "It wasn't so bad when we were connected, was it?"

The brother says, "No. We only thought it was bad. It wasn't bad. This is bad. Back then, we didn't know bad, did we? We only thought we knew bad."

The brother says, "Would you take it all back, if you could? Do you think we'd be better off if we were still connected?"

The brother says, "At least we'd be together."

The brother says, "But we are together. Can't you see that?"

The brother says, "At least we have that."

The Beast, A Clarification

We have never seen the beast, but we have heard about it. We don't know if it really exists, but we are afraid it does.

We have asked storytellers about the beast, and their stories range from the absurd to a realism more real than reality. We are told the Imperial Council created this beast, just in case someone ever found the secret passageway leading to the underbelly of the moon. We are told this beast was made from the scraps of other beasts, so every time it is seen, it looks different because it had so many parts competing for attention. We are told it has three thousand sets of eyes, some matching, most not, many of them scabbed over, unable to see. We are told these eyes sense movement through changes in air, that quite often, these useless eyes see better than our own functional eyes. We are told this beast has small parts from every beast on earth, that the Imperial Council called a gathering of all beasts and slaughtered them, and before the carcasses had a chance to cool, they carved away the integral parts, throwing the left over scraps in a large pile. We are told this pile of discarded pieces grew a spine out of anger, out of spite for the Imperial Council and all man, and hid itself before the Council knew it existed.

This hiding beast causes most nightmares. This creature hidden in some labyrinth, scheming the demise of man, deserves our fright. This self-created beast has a determination that does not negotiate, it's a beast with revenge etched in its mind and it cannot be stopped. So if it is true, if this thing exists, we are scared for dear Sylvester, stashed away in a maze no one has even seen, a maze that even its creator cannot crack, and its creator, he is caught in a labyrinth of his own with another beast, a heartless monster breathing sewer breath.

We are told the Imperial Council molded a beast and hid it in the moon, a beast with three thousand eyes and four million talons, a beast with venom and six hundred fangs, a beast lacking heart and brain. We are told this is the way the Imperial Council planned it because they did not want a beast that could feel kindness or weakness.

Now we can see how far folklore will stretch, how our storytellers exaggerate. And so we must tread closely to their ear if we are to believe them, we must unravel bits of truth from truths extended like taffy. For instance, there is one storyteller who says these beasts are nothing more than anxieties of an impending war, that there are no physical beasts at all. Beasts, of course, being metaphorical.

The Traveling Family

They are a family traveling with great purpose but no direction. They move because it's necessary, inching ever closer to where it is they need to go. They wander because they must.

They are a family that moves with laughter and joy, a family recently reunited and on a mission. They are a family in a car; the man is behind the wheel and the two women sit in the back, giggling like farting schoolgirls, and the man, conscious of the smell, smiles.

But the car does not move.

They are traveling, going forth, and the car does not move.

The stationary vehicle watches a slideshow of movement and weather, foliage blowing into clean white sand without blemish. The family occasionally looks out the windows and sometimes, one will mention how beautiful something out there is, but just as quickly, there is laughter again, and motion is forgotten in these bursts of uncontrollable emotion.

They know, this family, that soon, the scenery will be stagnant and when that happens, they will have reached their destination, and when this moment comes, there will be no more time for laughter and joy. There will only be seriousness and the entire fate of humanity dependent on them, this happy family.

Certainly, in such a dire time, most families would be strategizing, coming up with plans and back-up plans, but this family, they laugh and fart and simply smile.

Threesome

Yes, at first, Edward was dissatisfied with Emily. At first, their relationship was more like an arranged marriage with unreasonable expectations and romanticized and demonized notions of a future together. And poor Edward had fantasized about Emily for so long, from before he sang his song of sadness, since before she pried her eyes open with her talons, since before he'd even seen her up close, he'd imagined what their love could be. And now, Emily just seemed pathetic. Anything she did was a disappointment.

If Emily sang a song for Edward, he found her pitch wavered and she was slightly off-beat. If she braided his hair, he would find strands floating loosely in the water or even worse, the entire braid would be lop-sided. If she let her toes intertwine with his, her talons would puncture his skin. Everything Emily did frustrated Edward.

But only for a while.

Before long, Emily became family, much like Edmund was family, and the three of them did everything together. They slept together and played together. They enacted revenge together. They made love together.

Now to modern man, this certainly seems unnatural, but there was a closeness in the three of them that wasn't there when they were coupled. It was almost as if the addition of the third, the inclusion of the twin brother as a unit, created the closest bond possible between three humans.

Of course, this was momentary, but not because it could not be maintained. If there had not been war, if the Evolution Council and the Imperial Council had not manipulated the human species, they would still, to this day, have their perfect relationship. But this was not the case. There was a war, and in this war, they were killed. We know that the Ed brothers barricaded their bodies before Emily, attempting to shield her, and when they fell, when they died, she willed herself to death, placing her body between their rib cages, hooking her arms in theirs and silently falling asleep.

Creation

It is hard to believe that despite their overwhelming influence on the state of the world, Emily and the Ed brothers ended as carcasses like any other. They were thrown in a pile that sunk down to the center of the earth, and they rotted just like any other bodies.

Their bodies, so filled with the hotness of love and rage, spun with the corpses of other mermen and other men and other humans, and together, they created the core of the earth. Together, they let their hotness mold, and their bitterness and anger permeated the ocean with salt, and the thousands of bodies layered on top of each other, crammed so tightly air could not even form pockets, swirled with gravity to make mud, which the sun cooked into red clay.

Many today believe a story about a god who took his hands and formed man from clay, but the truth is clay was made from man. Dirt was created from decay, from the demise of man.

Before the First Story

Back before the daughter was born, the father waited until his wife was asleep, and when he saw her breath move in the calm of silence, he bent his mouth close to the fetus. His hand cradled her body and whispered a story into her unformed ears. He told her that two decades later, they would meet again, and he would forgive her for killing him, that she should be unafraid. He told her she needed to maintain strength, to build her focus to help her brothers, that not all revolutions end with death. He told her this as a preface to the story, a private conversation between father and daughter.

We shouldn't be surprised that the daughter is willing to share these most intimate details, while the story itself, the part we are most interested in, about that, she refuses to say a word.

Contact

Before her brothers left on their journeys, Sylvia warned them of dangers lurking when they were most calm. She warned them, but she was careful to not fate it to happen. Of all people, Sylvia Sylph understood that often, what she imagined in her head quickly manifest as truth. So instead, she relaxed her eyes and asked the Evolution Council what they knew of the beasts.

When no clear response came, Sylvia became frustrated, and in her frustration, she did something no one, not even a Sylph, could have ever thought up: she contacted her father.

Sylvia Sylph relaxed her father and asked him what he knew of these beasts. Even though Stanley Henklemeyer knew about his daughter, her relationship with Chloe, the lingering danger trailing his sons, and his wife's downfall into alcoholism, he was happy to see her. Stanley Henklemeyer knew his sons had separated, and overjoyed as he was at this sudden evolution, he kept his distance. But when his daughter, his killer, asked for his help, he was altruistically honest. He told her everything he knew of the beasts, which was not much. He explained how some thought the beasts were real, a melding of every beast that had ever lived on the earth, but others believed the beasts were metaphors, and though a monster with two thousand eyes sounded terrible, it was only one thing, a thing with many vulnerabilities, but a metaphor, he explained, well, that would be much worse. He said his sons were strong, but no one man, no matter how seeped in power and history, can defeat a whole army of mermen.

Faulting & Waiting

Stanley Henklemeyer was a man of many faults. Even so, there was a time, a time not so very long ago, when we thought the world of Stanley. We thought he was the kindest man around, a real hero, but obviously, we had misjudged.

It is true we wanted great things for him, and we were very disappointed when he committed suicide, but we didn't take it too personally, although certainly, we didn't want him to be so weak as to let a fetus take his precious life. And it's true we didn't like the way he groveled at Susan's feet, begging her to let him follow her, like a slave, like a prophet should never do, but she did save his life, even though she also played a large part in his death.

We cannot wait until the moment when we meet them all face to face. We cannot hold our breath long enough waiting for the Henklemeyer clan to come to us, their Evolution Council, and beg us to help them save their Sylph family. And it is approaching, this moment, and we can't wait. We have built ourselves thrones elevated to the height of gods so we may heartily laugh at them in their smallness as they come and plead their case.

It should not have come to this. We loved you, Stanley Sylph, but now you are no longer a Sylph, and when you changed your name, our feelings changed too. But don't worry, dear Stanley, there are ways you can redeem yourself. We're just not sure you'll appreciate your other options.

But mostly, we are interested in his daughters. Yes, we want to see Stanley humiliated, but we have never seen the true form of martyr, infinite in all her martyr traits, and his Sylvia is the rawest form of prophet, the closest to how they used to be when they ruled the earth. Although Stanley and Susan may be prophets, they are nowhere near as powerful as their progeny. These two girls, they are the key to the Evolutionary Revolution. So we wait. We wait for the reunification, for the collision, the war.

The Arrival

In the car, there is so much laughter and happiness, the family does not want it to end, even though an end is always inevitable. They would like to prolong this moment, but it is impossible. Moments last only as long as they last. You cannot elongate them, not even with a car full of prophets.

But before they open their car doors, they close their eyes, and together, they make this a positive experience. They change fate. They take away our thrones and our ego. They make us help them.

Hiding Place

In those years directly after the Evolutionary Revolution, the Evolution Council hid. They did not want to hide, but they had no choice. Although they had armies of their own, man killed without concern. Man rampaged the ocean. They climbed over each other reaching higher and higher into the atmosphere. They lusted for blood. They killed anything. They killed everything. They didn't care if it was animal or human or even plant. Nothing was safe.

To this very day, we are unsure how they managed not to kill each other, how they just stopped one day, a random day, they simply stopped murdering and began to rebuild. It is also unclear how and where the Evolution Council hid. In the years directly after the Evolutionary Revolution, the earth was still solid liquid. It took decades for the corpses to melt and form the core and nearly a century for that core to form land. It is said that the Evolution Council hid under the surface of the moon, in the labyrinth. It is said that the Evolution Council searched for the tree, but this cannot be proven.

Although it is possible that they hid under the moon, it is an unlikely scenario. The moon was dying. Its body was shriveling from malnutrition, and there were many quakes that cut deep serrated lines into its flesh.

Others claim the Council assumed the shape of man and lived among them, disguised. This possibility frightens us the most. If the Council had become man, then man's characteristics would have seeped into their essence, which would mean that we, their progeny, are as flawed as man, as weak and cruel as man, as equally to blame, as guilty as everyone else.

Hiding Place, Part II

And our forefathers hid. They hid as though they were powerless. They tucked their bodies beneath surfaces, forced themselves to forget who they were, and in those days directly after the Evolutionary Revolution, our forefathers watched from shadowed corners as man tore the earth into slivers and shards, looking to kill. Man was insatiable. It seemed, in fact, as if they absorbed the need for revenge from the mermen they killed, as if anger could be transferred in death through osmosis. Passively, our forefathers observed man's destructions, his habits.

Of course, this is a time we are not told about. This is a time we must decipher through strings of indistinguishable words we were not meant to hear. It is a time begging to be forgotten.

But we can't. We are obsessed with their destruction, how they were so silent, so weak, when they could have fixed the earth with so little effort. We cannot understand how it came to this point, how we are here, in this place that does not accept us because it does not accept our past, our history.

We, however, do know the Evolution Council eventually re-emerged, but this was much later, a century or two after the revolution. But the Council was not the same. They did not make decisions so easily, so apathetically. Every decision was deliberated and debated for years, and even then, they often stale-mated, so nothing would happen at all. And meanwhile, man had forgotten about the Council's existence, and so to this very day, we hide. We hide like our forefathers hid. But we are not ashamed. We do this because it what we have always done. We hide out of habit. We hide with our army of hundreds of poets and storytellers. We hide even though our egg is safe, and once it hatches, we will never need to obscure our eyes from the eyes of man again.

The Father and Daughter Make Nice

Stanley Henklemeyer was vacuuming when it happened. He was vacuuming a rug, and although it wasn't a large rug, it required his utmost care and attention. Stanley Henklemeyer vacuums in a checkered pattern. First horizontally, then vertically, and when he's completed a perfect series of perpendicular intersections, he undoes his obsessive-compulsion with clean diagonal sweeps. He is careful not to let his sloppy footsteps touch his work.

But he was in the middle of his columns when he heard it. It was soft but clean, ringing of desperation and family.

It said, "Papa?"

It pleaded, "Papa? Please."

Stanley counted where he was in his vacuuming and responded, "Yes dear. Yes, my Sylvia. I'm here."

The daughter said, "Papa, I'm sorry. I'm sorry about what I did."

The father said, "You had to. You had no choice. If I were stronger, I would've helped."

The daughter said, "And now you're indebted to her because I was too weak."

The father said, "We had no choice."

The daughter mourned, "We had no choice."

He said, "Is Betty treating you kids OK? I was worried about leaving you with her."

She said, "She's nothing I can't handle, but Papa, there are so many things that are worse than Betty, and Eliot and Sylvester, Papa, they're in trouble, and I can't help them, and Papa, I'm scared. Please, help us."

He said, "Of course, dear. Of course."

She said, "Really?"

He said, "On one condition."

She said, "Papa, you should be ashamed of yourself, putting conditions on your own sons."

She said, "What condition?"

He said, "When this all happens, it'll be up to you and Chloe to save the boys. You can't be scared. You must be unafraid, and Chloe, she's not as strong as you. She doesn't have your powers. You have to help her. She is, after all, your sister, and I know you love her, Sylvia. I know you love her like you wish you could love me."

She said, "Papa, you're silly. She's my twin. I could never abandon her, not the way you abandoned us, but Papa, I understand. You had to go help her because she needed it more than we did."

He said, "My darling Sylvia, my daughter, my sister, I'm so sorry."

She said, "I know, Papa. I know."

The Secret Life of Eliot Sylph, Part II

Eliot Sylph has a secret, and now that he is caught in this cold maze, he wishes he'd told someone before he left. In the very least, he wishes he'd shared it with his brother, his best friend, his twin who used to be connected to him.

Eliot makes his way around the maze, using his x-ray night-vision to avoid hazardous paths, and as he walks, he thinks about his secret. He thinks about his secret and suddenly, he's scared he won't make it out of here. He'll die with this secret stuck inside him.

Eliot yells, "Sylvester! Can you hear me?"

He waits.

"Sylvester!" He yells, "Are you out there?"

Nothing.

Eliot lets his body collapse onto the slimy ground. He sits there with his soft brown hair curtaining his arms warm. He sits there, remembering how his papa was waiting for him that first night, as if he'd never left, as if he didn't die.

He whispers, "Papa, I miss you. Papa, why did you have to leave us like that? Why did you have to find me like that? Why did you make me do this? Papa, can you hear me? I'm scared. Papa, I'm scared I'm going to die like this, without Sylvester. All my life, Papa, I only wanted two things. First, I wanted you back. Second, I wanted to be a single boy, and Papa, why did you have to make both these things, these things I wanted for so long, why did you have to make them so terrible? Papa, this is all your fault."

Eliot whispers, "Papa, I hate you. Even if both me and Sylvester make it out of here OK, I'll hate you forever."

He waits.

And waits.

It's cold and he's shivering.

And just as if it's been no time at all, Eliot hears his papa say he's sorry.

A Change of Names

Stanley Henklemeyer makes Eliot warm. He takes away the darkness of the labyrinth. He blinks and the walls become permeable. He opens his eyes, and he's no longer a Henklemeyer. He's Papa Sylph again, and he watches as his son falls backwards into cotton candy walls.

He does this all while holding Susan's hand because he could not do it alone. Susan helps keep their family alive.

He does this while the Evolution Council watches.

He does this because they make him.

But also because he wants to.

Not that he can tell the difference.

Talk of Revolution

Sometimes, we have no choice but to laugh just a little because with all that is going on—the emergence of hundreds of poets and even more storytellers, an egg that flares hotter than stars, and prophets and two-headed boys and girls with wings sprouting from their thighs living together as families—humans still walk around the earth as if everything is as it ought be. They go about their day-to-day activities, pretending that they do not feel the earth warming, pretending they are not in danger. They check their e-mail, drive their SUVs, plan lunch dates on their Blackberries and iPhones, listen to their iPods. They litter and eat. They go to doctors and take medicine. They shop without looking at ingredients. They do not care what they put in their bodies. They do not care about their bodies.

Those with notions of historicity, they understand the peril of this moment, but men do not care about the immediate danger the Evolutionary Revolution will bring. No, the only revolution many people today care about is a revolution against their own boredom and made-up dramas.

Fog

Eliot Sylph falls backwards, through a layer of permeable softness, soft like cashmere, soft like cotton candy, and onto grass. Moments ago, Eliot was in a damp, disgusting concrete maze. Seconds ago, he used x-ray and night-vision to see. He used his last breath to curse his papa, and just like that, he was falling backwards onto grass that had not been there just a moment before. Now, sunlight hits his eyes something painful, and Eliot squints because it hurts and shuffles his hands into blinds. It takes Eliot Sylph a moment or two to adjust.

When he reaches equilibrium, Eliot stands. All around him, where there used to be walls, there are translucent barricades he can move through. They may as well not be there. Even better, Eliot can almost see through them. These new walls, they're tangible fog, and Eliot has always been keen on fog.

As a boy, back when he was a two-headed boy, Mama and Papa Sylph only let him and Sylvester outside when it was night and there was fog all around. The Sylph boys would play a game, lowering their lids until they were almost closed, tightening their field of sight, and they would see whose eyes could see the farthest. Eliot always won but only because he cheated.

Now, Eliot Sylph stands, a single boy, in a maze of fog walls, and he plays his game again. He pretends Sylvester is there, and he lowers his lids until his eyes are almost closed, until he can see a shimmering gold tree with gold leaves waving him forward.

The First Story, Part III

When Stanley Sylph was just a forethought in his mama's belly, his papa bent his mouth down past the skin and muscles and fat of his wife's stomach. His papa put his mouth right next to Stanley's ear and told him a story. It was the very first story Stanley Sylph ever heard.

This story was, in fact, the same story that Susan Henklemeyer's real papa told her when she was just a fetus, the same story that Chloe heard, the same story that Sylvia heard.

And this story, it was not an elaborate story of storytellers and poets. It was a story for prophets and prophets alone, and it was simple. It was only three sentences long, but these three sentences will change the entire fate of mankind.

The Very First Story

It is a mistake of definition.

We will complete the revolution to bring us back to where we first began. It is our destiny.

Hidden Beasts

Eliot Sylph knows there should be a beast in this translucent labyrinth. He is certain it exists, and with his almost closed eyes, he scans the maze, but as far as he can see, there is nothing but foggy walls and a golden tree. There is no multi-headed monster, no accumulation of all that is grotesque on the earth, there is nothing but beauty.

Eliot Sylph is no fool. Even as he makes his way toward the tree, he feels this isn't right, something is very wrong, but still, he can't help himself. The tree glitters brilliance, and he feels his body sift through walls, closer and closer to luminescence.

Sweat

It is not because Sylvester does not hear Eliot's call that he does not respond. Sylvester, in fact, wants nothing more than to answer his brother, his best friend, his twin who used to be connected to him, but he is in no state to do so.

Sylvester Sylph stands in his labyrinth, completely unclothed, drinking his own sweat, and still, he is hot. He cannot be sated; his hotness is overwhelming. Any movement brings intense waves of flaring swelter. For every ten steps he makes, he must stop and rest. Sylvester collapses onto the sweaty ground, but he is resolute. He knows he must make it to the egg, but he is tired and hot and he can drink his sweat by the handful. Sylvester Sylph closes his eyes, just to rest, just for a moment, and when he opens them, the salt from his sweat stings so he uses his hands like ladles to remove pools of bodily secretion from his sockets.

When he reaches equilibrium, Sylvester heaves his torso upright and right there, right in front of him, looms a thirty-headed, two-hundred-eyed, one-thousand-limbed creature, and it is pissed.

Stanley is Saved, Part II

The father says, "Let my boys free."

We say, "They are free. We've done nothing to trap them."

The father says, "I know your tricks."

We say, "You know nothing."

The father closes his eyes, and we fall to the ground. We fall from the heights of our thrones.

We say, "You know nothing. You have no power over us."

The father closes his eyes, and nothing.

The father closes his eyes, and when he opens them, we are back on our thrones.

The father says, "You don't know what you've done. You don't know what we can do."

We say, "You're nothing, you pathetic little prophet. You have no history, no notion of who you are or what you can do, and furthermore, you don't remember us. We would laugh at you, but you're not worth our laughter."

Still in the car, Susan Henklemeyer closes her eyes hard, and Stanley disappears. We know it was Susan who saved him. She is his perpetual savior, though even she cannot save him from the future we've prescribed.

Insurance Plan

Sylvia Sylph did not trap her mother in her room because she was cruel. Rather, she did so to ensure her whole family's safety. She knew her mama would interrupt her brothers. She knew her mama would get in the way so even when Sylvia Sylph let her mother go free, she made her drink a bottle or two of wine. As an insurance plan. Plus, it's nice to drink after being locked in a room for so long. Most mothers would.

The Scream, Part I

Yes, he's hot and yes, it's quite possible the heat's swarmed him for so long he passed out, but this beast, it's no hallucination. So Sylvester does what he knows how to do.

Sylvester opens his mouth as open as he can and screams.

He screams so loudly he scares himself.

He screams so loudly it penetrates place and time.

Sylvia, keeping watch on her brothers in one room and her mama in another room, feels the scream as though it were coming from her own throat. His sound vibrates her entire body. It is her duty to protect the family, to watch over her brothers' sleeping bodies as they alone venture into different lands, but Sylvester's scream cannot be ignored.

Sylvia blinks and her mother is sober again. Sylvia blinks and her mother understands the weight of the situation. Sylvia blinks, and she is gone, and it is just her mama, sitting with her two single boys, caught in slumber, trapped.

The Beast

The beast is huge. At certain angles, clouds rest softly against its tens of heads. At other angles, its teeth penetrate stars. But from behind, it's scarcely larger than five or six feet tall, though it is rare to see this beast from behind. Most often, you can only see the version larger than imagination, the version that makes even the bravest men cry.

The Scream, Part II

Yes, he's hot and yes, it's quite possible the heat's swarmed him for so long he passed out, but this beast, it's no hallucination. So Sylvester does what he knows how to.

Sylvester opens his mouth as open as he can and screams.

He screams so loudly he scares himself.

He screams so loudly it penetrates place and time.

Eliot, in his fog-filled labyrinth, feels the scream as though it were coming from his own throat. The sound vibrates his entire body, and suddenly, as if it had never occurred to him before, Eliot understands the immediacy of the situation.

Without even a pause, Eliot Sylph calls for his father.

He says, "Papa, it's me, Eliot, and Sylvester needs you. He needs help, and I don't know who else can possibly help him. We're a family, Papa, and we need you to make it."

Eliot is flustered. He speaks somewhere between sobs and slurs and screams, but he hears his papa's voice say, "It's OK, Eliot. It's OK, my boy. Just keep on going. It'll all be OK, just you wait and see."

So Eliot, quivering from the resonations of the scream, continues walking. He walks like he can't hear Sylvester, like he's deaf, like they're not even brothers.

Heartbrain

This beast with its hundreds of eyes scattered all over its body lacks both heart and brain, but it is overcompensated with excessive heads and eyes and talons. Without the self-knowledge to sufficiently understand this lack, this beast is filled with a nameless sadness.

Only Human

They are not as we imagined. We've dreamt of meeting these two families. We've devoted a great deal of mental energy envisioning this moment, this moment when we would see the Sylph and Henklemeyer families, how each character would look, how each subspecies would differ from our own reflection. But this is not the case. We sit here on our thrones, our thrones that the Henklemeyers had thought they'd gotten rid of, and yet, here we are, sitting on thrones so high we may as well be gods, and look at them. Look at Stanley and Susan. They look just like any other humans. Look at their pale brown hair. Look at their dry elbows. Look at their plain clothes. They're nothing special.

And Sylvia. Our precious Sylvia Sylph who came all this way just because her brother beckoned, she's pretty and young and delicate and human. We had expected greatness. We had expected a heroine. A real heroine, or in the least, we had expected more than this, yet, here we are, the Evolution Council with the very same blood in our bodies as the original Evolution Council, and we look down on our playthings, our toys, and we are forced to laugh, just a little. We look down and we see Chloe, a relic from a time when man was kind. We see her little red wings struggling against the air, kicking against gravity with all the ugliness they can muster, and we scoff.

Of course, there is some hope the Sylph boys will still be something special, but seeing their family, we doubt it. They probably were great back when they were still connected, back when they looked more like mermen, but now they are single and lost in the confusion of labyrinths, and we imagine that they, too, are nothing but a disappointment.

We do not intend to be cruel, but we have waited for this, and we are disappointed. We laugh because these mismatched people standing so small at the foot of our thrones, they are supposed to be the saviors, they are the ones who will bring about this great Evolutionary Revolution forecasted eons ago. They are supposed to be so much, but look at them. They're human.

The Moon's Death

It is said that the moon died because man devastated its soil with genetic manipulation, that in striving for the perfect tomato, splicing it with genes from elk and rhinoceroses and all those chemicals derived, not from the soil, but from the creative minds of men, eager to do less work, eager to make things better, they killed their moon, their home. It is said the moon was so saturated with man's poisons that its soil dissolved into a dust so fine it dug into skin's pores, and as it entered man's body, it multiplied colonies of toxicity.

It is uncertain whether the moon's death had anything to do with man's change or if we should solely blame the Evolution and Imperial Councils. All we know is the shift in man was so drastic, there must've been a fundamental chemical change.

It is said man killed the entire moon within just one generation—the generation of the first sexed men.

It should be mentioned that many disagree with our assessment of how man killed the moon, but they are certainly in the minority. They believe the moon lost its vitality the day the Imperial Council disbanded and left the Golden Tree to waste away in the middle of the moon. Of course, those are the very same people who believe that the Golden Tree offered man variegated flora, that man was not greedy, that man in fact tried to stop genetically modified organisms from spreading and infecting the entire moon like weeds.

Finger Pointing

It is not surprising that the Imperial Council wanted man to rule the world. With a name like the Imperial Council, it's what should be expected. What is surprising, even with all our knowledge and history, is the degree to which man exhibited his inhumanity, the pain he inflicted without reflection, without awareness, with complete comfort.

What is surprising is that the Imperial Council changed man with ease.

Okay, so the Imperial Council was not solely responsible for everything. It's true our forefathers, the Evolution Council of yore, played a role; however, it was a very small role. Yes, it was the Evolution Council who gave man sex and gender and three extra senses, and it was the Evolution Council who took away those three senses when it was most volatile, and of course, we cannot neglect how they made men immune to hydrogen, but still, these were made in hopes of improving man.

So yes, it's true the Evolution Council made some costly errors when dealing with man's evolution, but despite all their mistakes, nothing could compare to the Imperial Council's desire and ability to manipulate man into a monster, a more beautiful, aesthetic version of the beasts they'd created so long ago to protect their deepest secrets.

A Sylph Boy Receives a Task

The day the very first storyteller arrived, we were concerned, and as a Council, we entrusted our egg to Eliot Sylph to hide. Of course, he had no idea this was expected of him, or for that matter, that anything was expected of him. This is precisely why we chose him. We had, for some time, considered giving the task to Sylvester, but we found him too clever, too cocky. We were concerned he was wiser than we could trust, that he might try to outsmart us.

In retrospect, we get a good laugh out of it. The instant we trusted Eliot, he changed. We jovially giggle at how the moment we had faith in him, he manipulated his own conjoined brother, his best friend, his twin, so that he could be a single boy, if only for one night. And it is equally ironic that he chose to do what we did not have the nerve—the audacity—to do. To this very day, we enjoy a healthy chuckle when we think about how he took our egg, our precious future, and rather than worship it as we do or in the very least protect it, Eliot Sylph created an elaborate labyrinth that would obscure it and sent Sylvester to odyssey for it. All our deliberation and consideration as to which brother would be the most ideal candidate was ignored and undermined by a nonchalant, hormonal boy, eager to get outside, eager to forget a life of captivity.

Yes, of course we can appreciate the fact that we were the ones who gave Eliot the egg. We laugh because it is because of us that we are not on the verge of the Evolutionary Revolution, the true Evolutionary Revolution, and had we chosen Sylvester, everything would be quite wrong, quite contrary to this one particular moment with these very specific circumstances. We declare we made the right decision, the only one to be made.

Every Generation

Every generation or so, the Evolution Council deludes itself into believing that the Evolutionary Revolution, the one promised by the very last prophet, will occur in their lifetime, and as such, every Evolution Council labors to bring the prophecy into fulfillment.

In part, we understand and acknowledge the very unlikely possibility that we are no different, that we are just another Evolution Council waiting for a war that will never come, but there are some very fundamental and obvious differences between all those Councils who came before and us. First and foremost, we know prophets are not extinct and so the legend of the last prophet remains only a myth, although we certainly do not doubt he promised a revolution based on evolution that would change the entire course of the earth. Secondly, no Evolution Council in the past has accumulated or amassed such a large number of storytellers and poets. Thirdly, we have the egg that promises a revenge, an egg so heated it has caused most of global warming, though this does not excuse man's horrendous treatment of the earth. Finally, it is our duty as the Evolution Council to further the belief in the Evolutionary Revolution, to perpetuate the dream of a world as pristine as we have never known. This belief is coded in our psyches. We imagine this world, and all we see is war.

A Soft Moment

And the mother said to the fetus inside her, "It was a mistake in definition. We will complete the revolution to bring us back to where we first began. It is our fate."

Brethren

Sylvester screams so loudly the beast's ears collapse, and this poor pathetic monstrosity of a beast shifts first to his left and then to the right and so on and so forth, this back and forth rocking for what seems like hours to frightened Sylvester, still screaming loudly, until the beast stops movement and stands flat-footed, fully balanced, and Sylvester, seeing this, hurtles a series of sharp shrills at him, and the poor beast falls over. He falls flat on the part of his body that could be a back if only he didn't have all those superfluous limbs and eyes and venomous fangs.

Sylvester Sylph watches with regret as this beast attempts to negotiate gravity and synchronized movement, and he is suddenly reminded of the way he and Eliot would spar for control of this or that bodily movement, how it felt when finally, after decades of powerlessness, of disenfranchisement, how it felt when he finally gained autonomy over his own body. Sylvester watches this beast, and he sees they aren't so different, this beast and this man. This beast and this half merman, this divided human.

So Sylvester stops screaming. He stops screaming and calmly reassesses the situation. He is in a maze, making his way toward an egg that could hold any number of things, most probably very living and very aggravated, and this thing, this beast of a creature has fallen at the sword of his scream, and this poor beast of a creature remains struggling on the grass, unable to do anything more than flounder his hundreds of arms and legs and wings and talons, his thousands of eyes filling with a clear mucous. He is caught vulnerable and powerless in the cage of his body, all for protecting his home, for fulfilling his purpose.

It is in this moment of sympathy and empathy Sylvester pretends he is Sylvia and smashes shut his eyes, and with his closed eyes, he wills both of them, both these freaks of the earth, these brethren of beasts, to stand before the Evolution Council. He closes his eyes to dissolve the maze and the task and the present and the future. He closes his eyes to change fate.

And on his own, he opens his eyes anew.

Superhuman Sylph

Even though Eliot is worried about his brother, this doesn't stop his quest to reach the Golden Tree, and even though he affectionately calls it the Golden Tree, he does so only because, by coincidence, it is both golden and a tree. He has no notion of history, no concept of legacy. He has no idea that the future of the earth lies hidden in this tree.

Eliot continues to sift his body through walls, slowly making his way toward the tree. He is not rushed, and he is not concerned. Right now, he is immune. He can change solid into gas. He can see what should not be seen. He is superhuman. He can speak to those no closer than a full planet away. So cocky Eliot keeps walking. He skips onward, penetrating the moon as if its death was a playground.

Of course, ever so often, Eliot pauses to calibrate his heartbeat to his brother's, checking that he is safe. He counts his pulse and determines calmness, and when he is satisfied with both, he continues his odyssey, letting nothing but Sylvester slow his mission.

Repetition

It is no coincidence that man today has defaulted into the same patterns as before, that he is killing the earth as he had killed the moon, only this time, there is no one above man pulling strings to make him act as he once acted. No, this time, he's doing it on his own, as if he had no sense of history, no sense of his own legacy as the exterminator of his brothers and foes.

Today, there is no moon left. It is a shell of dust, and we cannot even imagine what will happen to the earth once man is done this time.

We think back, back through the memories of poets, and we see how even at the cleanest we have ever experienced the earth, it is nowhere near the way it was.

And for this, we are sad.

And we are scared.

Certain Differences

We are certainly unlike any other Evolution Council of the past, if only because we have poets and storytellers at our disposal, if only because we have all these puppets, these prophets and mermen pretending to be men, and if only because they have known nothing beyond what they are. They are sad and flawed and almost too ordinary.

A New Creation

Sylvester, taking hold of the monster's myriad hands, looks at the Evolution Council and says, "This here beast, he is a man. He is a new species of man, and you must accept him for who he is. You must give him a new name.

"And if you refuse my request," he continues, "I will bring the egg. I will bring it here and unleash a war, and we will watch you suffer as we have suffered."

The First Touch

It was Sylvia of course. It was Sylvia Sylph and the sister she never had, the sister she's wished into existence.

The moment Sylvia Sylph and Chloe Henklemeyer saw each other, the moment they made real person-to-person eye contact, poets and storytellers began to buzz, and their buzzing excited Chloe's wings, which began flapping all on their own, flapping with an intensity that Chloe had never seen, and though they were far away, at least a mile or so, Chloe's little raw wings flapped hard and lifted her above all the poets and storytellers, lifted her into the atmosphere above, bringing her ever closer to Sylvia.

The moment Sylvia Sylph and Chloe Henklemeyer first touched, it was love. It was as if Chloe's wings delivered her wholly into Sylvia's arms.

But this was nothing inappropriate. It was gentle and beautiful, an embrace that made the whole earth glow, if only for a few moments. It was the uniting, the beginning of something new, something unexpected. It was the first meeting of best friends, sisters, twins, and in this moment, everyone, even the Evolution Council, knew the world would never be the same again.

Caught

Eliot doesn't rush. This trip is a burden. It is something he must do, not because he wants to or even cares about it, but because it is required.

Eliot is not selfish, per se, but maybe it's because he was attached to Sylvester for so long, maybe it's because for so long, he had no control whatsoever over his own life, maybe it's because he was displayed like a freak for the world to touch in wonder and amazement at his body, his deformity, maybe it's because he was forced to rebreathe the air he and Sylvester had exhaled over and over in that cramped car trunk as they drove from city to city from house to hospital to carnival, or maybe it's because his father killed himself, or maybe it's because his whole family is unnatural, they're abnormal, they don't fit in with the rest of the world, or maybe it's none of these reasons at all but for some other completely unrelated cause, but either way, Eliot Sylph doesn't want to be here. He doesn't want to be forced to make his way through this stupid maze that's all hot and dark and wet, and he doesn't even want to reach the stupid fucking tree except that he knows that once he does, he'll be able to leave this stupid-ass place. But even more, Eliot Sylph doesn't want his brother, his best friend, his twin, the man who used to be attached to him, Eliot doesn't want anything bad to happen to him.

And Eliot realizes he can't help Sylvester until he is out of this maze.

But this doesn't make him walk any faster. It doesn't make him desire to finish. Eliot's caught in this maze of ennui and nihilism, where even though he knows he needs to get to the prize at the center, he doesn't do a damned thing about it. He just keeps on walking, stopping periodically to check on Sylvester, but by now, he's safe and he's calm, so really, Eliot's got no reason to rush.

A Bout of Laughter

It is a party, a celebration, only there is nothing to celebrate and all the guests are unwanted, undesired, foul. We, from our thrones, we look down at the humans gathered at our feet. We look at poets and storytellers, each one madly verifying and telling and orating and no one listens to these fantastical tales anymore. We look at the family of freaks—missing all but one—a family of prophets and divided mermen and man from so long ago, man back in the time when she was a kind, blind, winged creature. We look down at their blood, so mixed and mingled that they are no longer pure, we see how the traits of one have bled into the other, how they gain new powers through concentration. We look down and see Sylvester Sylph with this beast, this hideous creation without heart nor brain, yet somehow, it stands gentle as a feather, straight and aristocratic.

And we know we shouldn't, but this cacophony of voices offends our ears, so we laugh. We should have a different reaction, but the sound tickles us and we are forced to laugh.

We look down, and Sylvester's face is a large tomato and we laugh louder and harder.

We look down, and the Sylphs and Henklemeyers circle a clan and the beast opens its hundreds of mouths shooting venom and it is too much for us. We can't hold it in. We laugh until our sides hurt and we think of the millions of calories we're losing in these moments of intense hilarity, and just this thought makes us guffaw even more, and we have no control over this, we can't stop it, we think perhaps someone has poisoned us with laughing gas, and just this thought makes us guffaw even more, and we have no control over this, we can't stop it, and we think perhaps someone has changed our chemical composition because we are weak and this weakness makes us laugh further and further until we can hear nothing at all but our own voices, and tears blur our vision, and we can barely see our Sylphs and our Henklemeyers and our thousands of poets and storytellers disappear right in front of us and this magician's act, it's hilarious, so we laugh and we laugh and slowly, the laughter that hits us right in the gut slows into chuckle, then giggles, and we are little girls giggling behind our paws embarrassed because we have just lost it. We've lost everything. Just like that.

And still, we laugh because we have nothing else left to do.

Nihilism

Eliot doesn't consider himself a nihilist. He thinks himself above such trivialities because, after all, he has had a difficult life. He's known more than most people. He's smarter and wiser and he's known suffering, and for those reasons, he's above nihilism. But if this is the case, why doesn't he hurry? Doesn't he want to reach the end?

Eliot ambles along and wonders why he isn't more concerned. He has no answers, just movement, so he keeps walking with no particular motivation, with no end goal, just movement for the sake of movement.

A New Friendship

With beast in hand, Sylvester returns to the exact spot they left in the maze. With the beast in hand, they skip along the path, gaily whistling this or that tune. Yes, it's still hot, but they don't mind. They continue on their way, as if their new friendship can cool all revengeful desire radiating from the egg, as if they can't feel the egg's temperature, as if camaraderie can dampen even the most heated of passions.

The two of them skip and do cartwheels and somersaults along the path. They hold hands and spin each other around in tight circles. They smile and laugh, sharing the most intimate of secrets, until the moment we've been waiting for, the moment this half-merman and this beast stand in front of the magical egg, an egg flaring hotness that bursts rage in puffs of steam.

And just like that, their hands release from each other and they remain as they have always remained: individual and alone.

Historical Moments

We are not befuddled, but we don't like what has happened. Certainly, it was expected. Nay, it was forecasted. We knew from the very beginning those sisters would try to be heroines, that they would at some point connect with each other and from that point on, they would be impenetrable, impossible to defeat.

We think perhaps this is the way the Evolution Council so long ago reacted when they first saw Emily fall from the sky, when they first realized how this fallen man, caught deep in the clear, clean ocean, would be that metaphorical straw that would destroy the order of things, that perhaps if only Emily hadn't heard Edward, that maybe, just maybe, the Evolutionary Revolution would have never happened, that the Earth would remain as it had always remained. But the fact is that Emily did fall, and the Ed brothers did fall in love with her, and war did ensue, and the world is changed, and so when we witnessed Sylvia and Chloe meeting, we knew it was one of those moments, just like the connection of Emily's wings with the surface of the ocean, this was a moment to be remembered.

The Revenge of Memory

All those dead bodies huddled together in the middle of the earth, gravity pushing them tighter, more compact, and the movement of the man swimming circles around and around increasing the rotation, and the sun melting all that flesh, all that rot, and from all of this, we have the core of our earth, a core that on occasion, remembers its history, the pain from which it was derived, and its rage pushes through layers and layers of mantle and rock and soil and history up to the surface, and by the time that anger reaches the surface, it burns even the thickest and strongest of man's creations into ashes.

The Golden Tree, Part II

Steady movement accumulates, and after all of Eliot's movements are added together, he reaches the Golden Tree. Even though it's dormant, the tree is a bright star, and for a moment, just one evanescent moment, beauty completely blinds Eliot Sylph.

The Army Arrives

Eliot Sylph shields his eyes with his right hand until it is dark again, and when his vision readjusts, the tree is gone. The tree is gone, but he can still see its radiations. The tree is gone, but where the tree was, there is an army of people. Eliot Sylph takes a moment, thinking perhaps this is an illusion, something he's miraged into existence. But no, as far as he can see, there are people of all sizes and shapes, but between the cracks of their bodies, the glow of the tree remains. It emanates through flesh, making everything a little more majestic.

Ignorance

When the mermen sang their song of revolt, the Evolution Council was overjoyed. They thought they were witnessing the very beginnings of revolution, the masses joining together to raise a singular voice of discontent with the order of things, of life, of their subordination and pain.

The Evolution Council watched as mermen protested, their fists rising toward the sky, pumping constantly upwards, up to where they wanted to be.

Of course, the Evolution Council was hardly prepared for direct action, if only because it was not like mermen to be so active in their desire for change, if only because they'd forgotten or failed to notice that there was a man in the midst of all those mermen, if only because they, the infamous Evolution Council, had forsaken the immense authority of love.

Because they were ignorant, they weren't prepared for all that ensued. It was because of this ignorance that the war that followed was not a revolution based on evolution. The war was simply a war. It was not a revolution, for the mermen's anger was assuaged when they forced their bodies to separate, and as for evolution, well, what happened was not evolution. It was a democratic decision that, by mere coincidence, dealt with a physical altercation in form.

A Speculation

No one knows what happened to the Imperial Council after the Evolutionary Revolution, but some say they simply dissolved into the chaos of war's aftermath. They disguised themselves as ordinary men, doing ordinary tasks, keeping their heads low lest someone recognize them. It has been said that the Imperial Council, much like the Evolution Council, never truly died, but unlike their counterpart, the Imperial Council did not hide. They disguised themselves but not in shame. It was a strategic move, and as such, we fear they may, at any moment, reappear to devastate the revolution we can almost taste.

We hope this speculation is wrong. We hope they died like their precious Golden Tree. We hope.

Poets & Storytellers

When asked about the Imperial Council, a storyteller said, "There was never any Imperial Council. They whole thing was a myth, a story to make the Evolutionary Revolution all the more divisive and cruel."

A poet responded, "Once, there was a tree."

A storyteller retorted, "Trees grow only where there is precipitation. Without adequate precipitation, trees cannot form."

A poet yelled, "I have seen! I have seen!"

When asked what happened to the Imperial Council after the Evolutionary Revolution, a poet said, "It never happened."

Another poet said, "There were so many corpses, such a terrible smell. After the revolution, you couldn't decipher rat from human. There is no way to know what happened to them, but I say, I saw these reflections in the eyes of some men glittering gold."

A storyteller said, "Trees cannot be made of gold. There was no Golden Tree. No Imperial Council. No Evolutionary Revolution."

A poet declared, "I have seen the Golden Tree with my very eyes, and at the meetings held at the Golden Tree, the Imperial Council planned to rid the world of all other types of human except man. At these meetings, I recorded their schemes, and though I want nothing more than to be able to forget, I can't purge myself of it. These memories, they get caught here, right here as I try to cleanse myself."

Another poet declared, "I have seen the Golden Tree with my very eyes, and it was not in the center of the moon and the Imperial Council did not meet there. The Golden Tree was a meeting place for drunkards and heroine addicts, a place for the commerce of sex and crime. If the Imperial Council met there, I swear they could not have discussed anything more than baby talk. They could not have formed words beyond gibberish."

A storyteller said, "There is a certain kind of wisdom in the way children speak. Often, it is misleading to believe there is nothing there."

Another storyteller interrupted, "You're no storyteller! How can what you said even be interpreted as a story? You're an imposter!"

Another storyteller yelled, "Imposters! Two storytellers not telling stories!"

A poet screamed, "They aren't storytellers! They aren't storytellers!"

And such was our struggle to distinguish facts from falsities.

And we miss this, this symphony of disagreements. We would never have thought this when we were surrounded by so many storytellers and poets, but now that the sisters have taken them away, we find the newness of silence quite lonely.

The Creation of New Beings

But today, there are no mermen, save for the Sylph boys, and today, there are no winged men flying in a sky so clean, save for Chloe Henklemeyer. Today, there are men and women caught in the boredom of individualist capitalism. There is no revolution coming, not for them at least. These humans today, they aren't like those before them. We forget sometimes, watching our soap opera unfold, that what we see, these are abnormalities, freaks, and most people in the real world, they don't care. Most people, they are nihilists. And so if we are to hope for an Evolutionary Revolution, it will not come from the people. For a true revolution, we will have to create new beings who are not so bored, so undeniably post-modern in their approach to the doomed state of the world that they cannot see things falling apart, the earth losing its thin layer of transparent cashmere that protects man from the sun, from the rest of the universe. Man today cannot see all the destruction and pain. They live their menial lives, selling time for money, using money to buy more time, even though it was established long ago, long before Sylvia Sylph ever lived, long before man walked upright, that time was not someone to be reckoned with. But that is a whole different story.

Yes, if we are to see our Evolutionary Revolution, or any revolution for that matter, we will have to make new creatures and beings, new lives and a new earth, something to incite the need for change that humans today just can't see.

The First Kiss

Their bodies splitting forth a path and Eliot has no choice but to continue. The radiations from the tree are so powerful that even with his eyes shut, they burn, and a thick mucous secretes from slits crammed so firmly together that they form small wrinkles.

And Chloe, our young heroine, understanding Eliot's disposition, pulls strands of hair from her own head, and keeping her body very still, her wings elevate her hands to the level of his face, and first, she sews shut his eyes, and then, very softly, she kisses him.

Blind

Eliot can only feel movement now. He cannot see, being so blinded by the beauty of light, being so caught in the motions of love. He cannot even see Chloe, with her ugly red wings, trying hard to keep a steady hand to save his eyes, trying to maintain calm.

Nothing

And the brothers reach out and the brothers touch.

And nothing.

The audience holds their collective breath. The myths of the world hinging on this one moment: the intersections of skin on history.

And nothing.

Another Brotherly Conversation

But it wasn't as though the Sylph boys didn't know all along that it wasn't necessarily their task to save the day. Sure, they wanted to be heroes, but when the moment came, they knew they would disappoint.

Right before the crucial moment, in their heads, the brothers had a conversation.

The brother said, "This isn't right."

The other brother said, "No, it's not."

The brother said, "We're frauds."

The other brother said, "We had no way of knowing."

The brother said, "Now what?"

The other brother said, "They're waiting."

The other brother said, "Now, we disappoint."

And the brothers counted to three, silently together, and reached their brother hands forth.

But before they touched their respective objects, they reached a singular epiphany.

The Heroines Emerge

The brothers turn to their audiences, one brother with an entire slew of sub-species of humans, each one eagerly chattering about the truth of the situation, and the other with a beast of man and thousands of mermen raising their hands upwards to crack the shell of their confinement, and they say, "Humans, we are not your heroes. We are not the ones to bring forth your revolution."

And the mob screams, "Who will then? If not you, then who?"

And the brothers say, "Calm yourself!"

And the mob continues, "Who? Who?"

And the brothers say, "They know who they are. Let them come forth."

The crowd is silent and still. The humans, thousands of them, are comatose with excitement, until two girls step forth, both beautiful, both stopping movement with their smiles.

A Soft Moment, Part II

Sylvia blinks, and Sylvester and the egg stand beside them.

Sylvia blinks, and the Evolution Council stands among the crowd, ever anonymous, ever the same as anyone else.

Chloe flaps her wings and rises into the atmosphere. She says, "I will tell you a story. It was the first story I ever heard. You all must listen, for I speak softly. You all must listen and understand that this is what the very last prophet meant when he spoke of the Evolutionary Revolution. This story has been passed down from generation to generation of prophets, chastised as we hid, fearful for our very existence."

Chloe lowers herself.

When she speaks, the sound comes out clean. When she speaks, it is with both her voice and Sylvia's voice. When she speaks, the entire world is silent and ready to listen.

She says, "It was a mistake in definition. We will complete the revolution to bring us back to where we first began. We will complete the revolution to bring us back to where we first began. We will complete the revolution to bring us back to where we first began."

And Chloe touches the egg, and Sylvia touches the Golden Tree.

Restoration

The poets and storytellers and mermen and man and prophets and even the Evolution Council chant, "We will complete the revolution to bring us back to where we first began. We will complete the revolution to bring us back to where we first began. We will complete the revolution to bring us back to where we first began."

Until the earth is dissolved of land and the ocean is purified of salt.

Until there is no more damage to the ozone layer.

Until the earth is restored.

Mama Sylph Awakens

It wasn't her fault she fell asleep. It was hot in that room, and her boys were just sleeping, and Sylvia did give her that bottle of wine to drink all on her own, but when Mama Sylph woke up, her whole world was gone and she was swimming in water.

Mama Sylph was sure this was a dream.

Then, she saw her boys, her Sylvester and her Eliot, joined together again, and Mama Sylph said, "Boys! You're back together! I always hoped you would get back together."

And her boys said, "Yes, Mama, we're back to the way we always were, the way we were meant to be."

And Mama Sylph looked around her and everyone had two heads so she reached to touch her neck, expecting to be like everyone else, but she had no one, and for a moment, just one brief moment, she was sad and lonely.

Mama Sylph asked, "Where's Sylvia?"

And her boys pointed, and their finger led her eyes to Sylvia and her best friend, who's also her sister, who's also her twin, who's also attached to her.

And before their mother had a chance to ask another question, they pointed their single finger at their father, who was happily conjoined with his half-sister and lover.

Betty yelped in excitement, more certain than ever of sleep.

$(p+r)^n$

Lily Hoang's novel *Changing* (Fairy Tale Review Press) received a 2009 PEN/Beyond Margins Award and her first book *Parabola* won the 2006 Chiasmus Press Un-Doing the Novel Contest. She is an Associate Editor at Starcherone Books and Editor at Tarpaulin Sky. She currently lives in Canada.

Anna Joy Springer has toured the U.S. and Europe as a singer for punk bands and with the legendary Sister Spit. Her first novel is *The Vicious Red Relic, Love*. Birds of Lace has published her novella, *The Birdwisher*. She teaches at University of California, San Diego.

Located in London having drifted from Belgium, **VD Collective** is a front (for Discreet Ventures in art DIY). Generally it stands for Variable Device and, in this instance, for Visual Duct. Vincent Dachy acts as the spokesperson of VD collective (vdachy@talktalk.net) and has had some *Tribulations* published by Les Figues Press.

TRENCHART Series of Literature

TRENCHART is an annual series of new literature published by Les Figues Press. Each series includes five books situated within a larger discussion of contemporary literary art; each title also includes a work of contemporary visual art in response to the book's text. All participants write an aesthetic essay or poetics; the first title in each series is the collection of these aesthetics, specially-bound in a limited-edition book available to subscribing members.

TRENCHART: Maneuvers Series

TrenchArt : Maneuvers
aesthetics

Sonnet 56
Paul Hoover

Not Blessed
Harold Abramowitz

The Evolutionary Revolution
Lily Hoang

The New Poetics
Mathew Timmons

Maneuvers Series Visual Artist: VD Collective

Become a subscribing member of Les Figues and receive all five titles in the TrenchArt Maneuvers Series.

LES FIGUES PRESS TITLES ARE AVAILABLE THROUGH:

Les Figues Press <http://www.lesfigues.com>
Small Press Distribution <http://www.spdbooks.org>

ƒ

LES FIGUES PRESS
Post Office Box 7736
Los Angeles, CA 90007
www.lesfigues.com
www.lesfigues.blogspot.com